THE
NOTORIOUS
ABBESS

THE

NOTORIOUS
ABBESS

Vera
Chapman

Edited by Robert H. Boyer
& Kenneth J. Zahorski

Academy Chicago Publishers

Published in 1997 by
Academy Chicago Publishers
363 West Erie Street
Chcago, Illinois 60610

Printed and bound in the USA.

First Edition

Library of Congress Cataloging-in-Publication Data

Chapman, Vera, 1898–
        The notorious abbess / Vera Chapman.
                p.   cm.
        ISBN 0-89733-387-X (hc)
        ISBN 0-89733-447-7 (pbk)
        1. Fantastic fiction, English. I. Title.
PR6053.H36N68   1997
823'.914–dc20   93-15629
                                                      CIP

CONTENTS ─────────────

CONTENTS

INTRODUCTION _____

In 1976, Bob Wyatt, then an editor at Avon Books, recommended Vera Chapman to us as someone whose stories we might wish to publish in a future anthology. He spoke fondly of his meeting with her not long before in London. She was, he said, elegant and energetic, in a long red cape: her conversation was crisp and witty and, at the age of 78, she was about to make her literary debut.

All three books of Vera Chapman's excellent Arthurian trilogy appeared in 1976: *The Green Knight*, *The King's Damosel*, and *King Arthur's Daughter*. The trilogy subsequently appeared in a single-volume edition entitled *The Three Damosels*. *Judy and Julia*, a children's book, appeared in England in 1977, followed by two works in 1978, *The Wife of Bath* and *Blaedud the Birdman*. *The Wife* is an extrapolation from Chaucer's *Canterbury Tales*; *Blaedud* brings to life a legendary king of Druidic England. It was also in 1978 that the Abbess of Shaston, protagonist of the present work, first appeared, in a short story entitled "Crusader Damosel," in our second anthology (*The Fantastic Imagination II*, Avon, 1978).

Following this prolific three-year period, Vera Chapman published relatively little. She wrote a second Abbess story for us, "With a Long Spoon" (*Visions of Wonder*, Avon, 1981) and contributed "The Thread" to our 1980 anthology, *The Phoenix Tree* (Avon). "Crusader Damosel" enjoyed considerable popularity, appearing in other anthologies both in the United States and England where it found an appropriate place in *Dragons and Warrior Daughters*, edited by Jessica Yates (Collins, Lion Tracks, 1989).

What explains her late start, her extraordinary output from 1976–78, followed by more than a decade of relatively little, if first-rate, work? Fortunately, Vera Chapman wrote a brief biography in 1977 which helps to answer these questions.

"I was born in 1898, in Bournemouth, Hampshire, England. I went to Oxford (Lady Margaret Hall) in 1918, and was one of the very first women to be granted full membership of Oxford University in 1919, to wear the gown, and to graduate in 1921. I married a clergyman of the Church of England in 1924, and my first married home was in Lourenco Marques, which was then Portuguese East Africa (Mozambique). I returned to England in 1925, and for many years lived in country vicarages. Shortly after the 1940 war, I worked in the Colonial Office as a student welfare officer. I have now been retired for many years. I live in a Council flat in Camden Town, London, and I have two children and four grandchildren.

"There are several reasons why I have not attained publication until so late in life: chiefly that although I always meant to write, I have had so many other things to do — and also that until recently, there has not been much opening for "fantasy" writing. I had to wait till the present interest in imaginative writing gave me a chance.

"I have certainly accumulated the proverbial rejection slips, enough to paper a room."

Vera Chapman was "discovered" when interest in fantasy literature reached its height in the late 1970s. This widespread popularity declined in the 1980s, especially for works which, although of high literary quality, would not necessarily attract large, quick sales.

But despite this, Mrs Chapman never lost faith in her Abbess — nor did we — and she continued to turn out an additional five pieces about this unique character. She linked them into an episodic novel, wrote a preface and eventually added yet another five chapters. We are delighted that the collection is now available.

By the end of this work, the Abbess of Shaston emerges fully developed. She is a blend of Chaucer's two most original female characters: the demure Prioress, Madam Eglentyne, and the vibrant Wife, Alyce of Bath, although there is more of the unorthodox Alyce in her. She is a woman of noble connections who entered a religious order because it was one of the few occupations in the twelfth century in which a woman could find a measure of independence.

Like the Wife of Bath, the Abbess is an early proponent of women's rights, reflecting Mrs Chapman's own early feminist views. The Abbess is devout (up to a point), and faithful to her own Rule, by and large. But she also has enormous curiosity which propels her into travels, both literal and fantastic: with her the reader meets real twelfth-century characters: popes and kings and queens, crusaders and Saracens as well as saints and angels, satyrs and mermaids and spirits of questionable repute. The Spirit of Evil itself appears in various guises.

We conclude with a brief explanation of how this book evolved: In 1981, as Vera Chapman's U.S. editors, we had suggested she write a volume of Abbess stories. She produced nine stories by 1986 and three more by 1990, for a total of twelve; at which time we entered into a publishing agreement with Academy Chicago which, happily, has now resulted in this splendid volume.

We are grateful to have had the opportunity of assisting Mrs Chapman with this work. We also wish to recognize the tireless efforts of Jessica Yates, Mrs Chapman's close friend, secretary and unofficial agent. And, finally, our thanks to Dean Robert L. Horn of St Norbert College for his continued support, and to Mrs Peggy Schlapman who typed several versions of this work, including the final one.

ROBERT H. BOYER
KENNETH J. ZAHORSKI
ST. NORBERT COLLEGE

I.
MONKS
AND
MERMAIDS ⎯⎯⎯⎯⎯⎯⎯⎯⎯⎯⎯⎯

On the edge of the tremendous Shaftesbury bluff
stood Shaston Convent, overlooking the wide country below. Its ruins are there to this day, and it has
played its part in history, but the historians are
curiously silent about its notable Abbess Hodierna,
who ruled there at the time of the Crusades. Many
convents at that time instituted their own Orders,
with their own Rules, and this was one of such, at
least during those years.

It was the Convent of the Order of Saint Evodias
and Saint Syntyche, and it reflected the eccentricity
of its founder and Abbess. Those that know Saint
Paul's Epistles will readily recognise that Evodias
and Syntyche are mentioned there with a special
wish that they would "be of one mind in the Lord."
Their Order devoted itself principally to the work of
composing differences among neighbours; and as
the name Evodias means "fragrance," a great deal of
stress was laid on cleanliness. Indeed, the frequent
baths were considered a scandal in that bathless era.
So much washing was looked upon by many as a
sinful pampering of the flesh; and to save the reputation of the Evodian Sisters, it was reported that

they stood up to their waists in the cold river while reciting their offices. The fact was that they stood not in a cold river, but in a warm tub.

But that was only a part of the eccentricities of the Abbess Hodierna, learned, resourceful and full of unexpected talents. See her now, in her restrainedly elegant parlour, interviewing the Abbot of Iona, who has come to her because he is at his wits' end.

"It's a mermaid, Madame," he said. "We have no peace from her in our house on Iona, neither day nor night — particularly at night. I fear greatly for the young brothers. Oh yes, and for some of the older ones, too."

The Abbess smiled.

"Is she so very attractive, then?"

The Abbot threw up his arms.

"Oh, Madame, if you could picture . . . not that we have seen her very often — just a few glimpses — but it's her voice, her voice. Every evening between Vespers and Compline, she comes to the seawall below the monastery, and sings — oh, sings like an angel. Or not always like an angel. Sings about things that, well, that a monk ought to forget. She goes on singing while we are saying Vespers, and interrupts us. I've seen some of the brethren falter and break off the holy words, to listen to her. Especially Father Patrick. Oh, especially my poor Father Patrick, the sub-prior. For she calls him by name, and seems to have a — a tenderness for him.

Sometimes, we know, she creeps up close to the chapel windows, and listens when he reads or preaches, and even gazes in. There's some have seen her, and they say she has tears in her eyes. For as soon as Vespers are over, she changes her tune, and cries out, 'Father Patrick! Father Patrick! Give me a soul! I beseech you, give me a soul!' And then for the rest of the night she howls like a dog, so that it makes our blood run cold to hear her. All night till day-break, calling upon Father Patrick to give her a soul. We cannot sleep."

"Poor Father Patrick!" said the Abbess thought-fully. "What does he say to it? How does he take it?"

"Oh, I assure you he gives her no encouragement at all. He is a very virtuous man, and stands firmly by his vows. And yet I fear for him. He's a sufficiently good-looking man, and not so old . . ."

"I see." She hid a smile with the corner of her veil. "And has he ever answered her?"

"Oh, many times. He has cried through the window-slits, 'Go, Mermaid, I cannot give you a soul. Only God can do that, and we know that He will do no such thing!' And at that she wails and laments, and beats with her webbed hands against the wall, for the rest of the night. And next day she is back again."

"Have you tried exorcism?"

"We cannot exorcise her, for I do not think she is an evil spirit. We have no form of exorcism for anything else. And, indeed, the learned Doctors of the Church do not seem to agree as to what she is — whether an incorporeal spirit neither blessed nor damned, or a mortal creature half woman, half fish. We don't know how to treat her."

"And so you come to me?" She turned her big expressive eyes on him. "But why to me, when your learned doctors do not help you?"

"Why, because — well, because, Madame, you have something of a name for resolving hard questions, like the Queen of Sheba of old."

"She *asked* the questions." Gently she corrected him.

"So she did. But I think she may have given the wise king some wise answers too. In short, Madame, we think you may have the skill to help us, and also the female's touch to deal with another female. Will you come to Iona?"

"With all my heart," she said, smiling.

"It's a long journey."

"Oh, no longer than to the Holy Land, and I love travelling."

"I've got a stout company to travel with us," he said, "and a comfortable litter to carry you."

"Thank you, but I'll ride."

And so they went up the length of England, and across the perilous Scottish border, and at last to

Oban, whence a ship must take them to the holy Isle of Iona.

"No," said the shipmaster at Oban, "I can't do it. My men wouldn't stand for it. Nuns are bad luck, everybody knows that. Clergy are bad enough" (with a look between reverence and audacity at the Abbot) "and everybody knows it's bad luck to sail with the long-haired people we don't name." (The Abbess smiled, being well acquainted with the ban against the word "woman" at sea.) "But nuns are both. It can't be done. There'd be a storm, and the ship would sink."

Nevertheless he kept his eye on the steadily rising pile of gold coins in the Abbot's hand.

"Oh, but it's a lovely day," said the Abbess, looking out over the silky blue water, where the breeze just breathed enough to lift her white veil.

"I can see your ladyship doesn't know the weather in these parts," the man said sourly. "Like heaven now, and in half an hour's time, like hell . . ."

He eyed the gold coins as the Abbot added one more to them.

"Oh, very well, but it's at your own risk."

"I'll pray for you and the ship," said the Abbess.

"Don't you do any such thing, Madame," said the shipman, with such alarm that the Abbot could not help but smile.

"He's afraid your prayers might be evil spells," he said to the Abbess behind his hand, as they went up the gangplank and boarded the clumsy little vessel that was to take them to Iona.

"The shipmaster was right, you know, Madame," said the Abbot. "We who live on Iona know how changeable the weather can be here. Not that we pay any attention to local superstitions."

What had been a soft, smoky haze around the horizon, between blue sea and blue sky, had rapidly swelled into a menacing slate-coloured cloud, and was now spreading across the zenith. Below it came an ominous drift of turbulent white. The ship rocked, as the waves swelled up and broke, and a sudden wind caught the rigging, the sails, the nuns' light veils, the monks' black flapping robes. The two nuns in attendance on the Abbess quickly fled below into such cabin as there was. After a minute's hesitation, the brothers attendant on the Abbot vanished below too. The Abbess fastened her mantle and hood more closely round her, and leaned against the mast.

"Won't you go below, Madame?" said the Abbot.

"Not I," she replied. "I don't feel queasy. But I soon would if I went down into that stinking hole."

The storm grew worse. Far off they could see the strange-shaped Isle of Staffa; the gale was rushing them toward it. The frail little ship creaked and wallowed, buffeted by the huge waves. The Abbot crouched on his knees by the mast, praying. Through the roar, the Abbess was aware of the shipmaster at her side.

". . . running on the rocks," she could make out, as the wind snatched his words away, ". . . nothing we can do . . . the Lord's mercy . . . it's the mermaid . . . seen her . . . following us . . ."

"Here!" the Abbess shouted into his ear. Dropping her mantle and veil, which whirled away from her into the wind, and slipping off her shoes, she stepped up to the bulwarks, where two seamen were clinging. "Here. I know I'm the Jonah. Throw me overboard."

"Lady! Lady!" The shipmaster tried to hold her back.

"Madame, for God's sake!" The Abbot, holding on to whatever he could, tried to crawl toward her on hands and knees.

"No!" she said, her voice clear and hard above the tempest. "You must throw me over. It's not right for me to throw myself. That won't do. You *must* throw me over."

(Perhaps, if the truth were known, it had crossed her mind that as a strong swimmer, she might have a better chance of survival in the open water than trapped in that box of splintering firewood.)

Without a word, for words were useless now, the two sailors took her and heaved her overboard.

As she struck the water she saw the mermaid, rearing up astern of the ship in the scoop of a monster wave. All round the mermaid was phosphorescent light, and she was very beautiful and very angry. Her hair was not golden but jet black with glints of green, and her eyes were yellow-pointed like a tiger's.

The Abbess struck the water, went under, came up again; and as she struck out, she shook off her garments. Then, suddenly, in another great wave, the mermaid was upon her.

"You!" she heard the mermaid shriek. "You wicked woman! I know why you are going to Iona! But you won't get there! I know. You're going to prevent *him* giving me a soul! A soul, a soul!"

And the mermaid's cold, sinewy hands closed round the Abbess's neck.

"You fool . . ." the Abbess tried to shout, but the tough hands were at her throat, and she was being dragged down into the crashing water. She caught a breath of air. "You fool, stop it!" Again those hands. She wrestled them with her own hands — and indeed the Abbess's hands were strong. And holding off that choking grip for an instant, she spoke a certain Word of Power.

At that, the mermaid's grip suddenly relaxed. The waves seemed to relax too, as if something had deflated them.

"You fool," the Abbess gasped out, herself clinging to the mermaid now, "stop that! Don't you
understand? You *have* a soul already!"

The clutching hands dropped from her throat.

"What did you say?" The mermaid's lips were
close to her ear; one hand went round her shoulder,
supporting her, but the Abbess could feel that cold
hand shaking.

"Yes — listen — you have a soul already. Let me up
and I'll tell you."

For answer, the mermaid scooped the Abbess
into her arms and carried her like a baby. It was a
very cold bosom to be held against.

Presently, the Abbess felt herself to be set down
on a beach of warm dry sand in some dark rocky
place. Above her she could see the vast roof of a cave.
She roused herself.

"Listen," she said to the mermaid, and spoke
another secret Word — one that gave command over
the creatures of water. "Go and save that ship and all
the people aboard her. Then come back and I'll tell
you about your soul. Not another thing will I tell you
till then, and do you want me to say the Word that
comes next?"

"Oh, no, mistress, I hear and obey," said the
surprised mermaid.

The sand was warm and comfortable; some vol-
canic power below kept it heated. Presently the

mermaid came back, and put into the Abbess's hands a well-stoppered flask of good warming liquor.

"All right," said the Abbess, sitting up in the sand. "Now listen. This is good stuff, where do you get it? Oh, perhaps I ought not to ask you. Never mind. Now about souls. My good mermaid, all that about *having* a soul is wrong. We don't *have* souls, as if they were a sort of extra limb. We *are* souls, and *have* bodies. You and I, and those seals out there, and those little fish in the pool below — we are all souls in one state of growth or another. We begin as little scraps of life, little sparks from the fire of God, and we grow, age after age, passing from body to body, each time becoming higher and greater. Each little spark of God's fire becomes an angelic thing some day. Though we slip back, and have to start again, many times.

"Look at that hermit crab down there. As he grows too big for his borrowed shell, he slips out of it, and goes and hides his nakedness a day or two — that's how the soul slips out of its body — and then, look, he takes another shell that fits him better, as it were another body, and so goes on till he outgrows that one again. So you and I. We take body after body, but the thing that lives and grows within, our real self, is the soul, eternal and deathless."

The mermaid listened with her great eyes fixed immovably on the Abbess.

.

"So. It is like that? And I *am* a soul?"

"Yes, my dear, you and I, and the seal and the hermit crab and all. But the monks don't tell you this. They don't know it. And if the monks knew I was telling you all this, they'd burn me for a witch and a heretic."

The mermaid clutched both the Abbess's hands in her strong, cold, webbed one.

"But it's true? That I *am* a soul, and will one day be a Christian like you and enter your Paradise? Will you swear to me that this is true?"

"No need for me to swear," the Abbess replied with a solemn look deepening in her eyes. "You have heard the Words of Power that I uttered, and I tell you I speak the truth, as well as I know it, before That Name. You can be sure, my dear."

"Oh!" exclaimed the mermaid, relaxing with a long sigh. "If that is so I am content. I can go back to the depths of the sea and live my life happily." Colour bloomed in her transparent cheeks. She picked up her gold comb and began to smooth her hair.

"And now," said the Abbess, "you need not trouble Father Patrick any longer."

"Father Patrick? Ah, the poor man. But he preaches so beautifully. I thought he was the one who might give me a soul. No, I needn't trouble him further. But I love his preaching. I should like to go on listening to him."

The Abbess frowned a little. "I think you should leave him alone altogether now. The poor man thought you had carnal designs on him."

"Carnal designs?" The mermaid laughed. "The poor dear man, he'd be no sort of lover. I have my Triton down in the depths, and what more could I want? Poor dear Father Patrick — oh no, I'll leave him alone if that's what he's afraid of. But I shall miss his beautiful preaching. Come now, it's near morning. I'll take you to the island. Your companions are all safe in their warm beds in Iona now."

So she gathered the Abbess up in her arms once more, and carried her through the waves, which were now smooth under the fading stars, and set her down gently on the white beach of Iona, and with many farewells she slipped into the sea.

So there was the Abbess, safe on the beach as the sun came up, with only one disadvantage — she hadn't a stitch of clothing.

She began to feel cold. Even covering herself with the sand didn't help much. It hadn't the warmth of the sand in the mermaid's cave. She shook the sand off again, and shivered.

Then just as the sun showed its first rays, a monk came down from the monastery to the beach.

"Hey there, brother," she called. "Help me!"

He gave one look at her, and bellowed at the top of his voice: "It's the mermaid! Oh, blessed saints preserve us, it's the mermaid!"

He averted his face from the dreadful sight and groaned as he ran. "Sitting on the rocks, as bold as brass, and as — as the Lord made sinful Eve — so help me, a sinful man . . ."

"Come back, you silly monk!" she called after him in her loud, clear voice. "I'm no mermaid. Haven't you eyes?"

He cast those scandalised eyes behind him for a second, and then turned and ran again.

"Of course I'm not a mermaid, you donkey. If you don't believe me, look at my legs."

"Oh, blessed Mary, shield me!" yammered the poor man.

"Stop running away," she ordered in her most commanding tone. "I'm the Abbess of Shaston, although I've got no clothes on."

The monk stopped running, though he still kept his back turned.

"The Abbess of Shaston was drowned," he insisted in shaky tones. "If you're her ghost, depart in peace." He tried to make the sign of the cross toward her without turning round, which was very awkward.

"I tell you, I'm no ghost and no mermaid! I'm a living woman, and very cold, and very angry. Look, you can get the whole community if you like, walking backward if they daren't look at me, so long as they bring me some clothes, and the warmer the better. Now go, and tell your Abbot *that*. And for the good Lord's sake, hurry up, or I'll be a dead fish soon enough if you don't."

Without any more perilous looks back, the monk scuttled off, and presently there emerged from the gate of the monastery a strange procession — the whole twenty-four monks, four abreast with the Abbot at their head, and their arms full of clothes, walking backward. When their feet touched the high water mark, as they ascertained by looking downward, they halted and threw the clothes on the ground behind them; then took a dozen paces toward the convent door.

The Abbess quickly gathered up what she could do with, and gratefully shrugged herself into the thick wool garments.

"My Lord Abbot, don't you know me now?" she said.

They about-faced, and saw her, a slim black figure, standing most decorously with a monk's long black robe cast about her, and the black hood drawn over her head.

There were rejoicings and congratulations, and of course devout thanksgivings.

"The mermaid will not trouble you anymore," the Abbess announced, her eyes resting on Father Patrick, who certainly was a personable young fellow, though doubtless not in the same class as a Triton. "I have persuaded her that she need not long for a soul, and that you, Father Patrick, could not in any case have given her one. But I think you should pray for her all the same. She admired your preaching, you know, but she was not enamoured of you. Make no doubt about that."

"No?" he said, just a little crestfallen.

"No. She's gone back to her own wedded husband, as a good woman — that is — as a good creature should. You will never see her or hear her again."

They all thanked the Abbess, and praised God for so great a deliverance.

"You can now sing Vespers and Compline in peace," she said.

Just one old monk lingered behind and spoke in a whisper to her.

"I'm sad at heart," he said. "We shall be lost without our mermaid."

II.
THE
WHITE
KNIGHT'S
GAMBIT

"I consider these tourneys," said the Sieur de Maltravers, "the best possible training for the war in the Holy Land."

He looked round with some complacency at the well-appointed tilting-ground at Westminster; he was there representing King Richard, now gloriously engaged in thrashing the paynims in Outremer. On his left, as he sat at the centre of the gorgeously draped grandstand, was the Abbot of Glaston, and on his right that lovely though doubtless sanctified lady, the Abbess of Shaston. Rumour had it that if those two, the Abbess of Shaston and the Abbot of Glaston, were to wed — scandalous thought! — their progeny would own more land than the King of England himself.

However, the present business of the Sieur de Maltravers was with the magnificence of the tourney, and to keep himself on good terms with those two powerful ecclesiastics. So he had better not let his thoughts stray to the impressive figure that the Abbess made. The robes of her Order hid and restrained her undoubted good looks, but added a certain attraction also: the softly folded white wimple across the forehead drew attention to that forehead's breadth and whiteness, and the fine line of the eyebrows; the gorget folded around the pure oval of the face emphasized its shape; the white habit of the softest wool, with a discreet flash of sky-blue lining, hinted at a graceful figure. The Sieur de Maltravers jerked his attention firmly back to his subject, and to cover his confusion repeated what he had said before.

"An excellent training for the fighting in the Holy Land."

"Now there I disagree with you," said the Abbess. "Jousting's a fine game, and I love to see it well done; but it's no sort of preparation for warfare in Outremer. If you'd nursed them, as I've done in the Hospitallers' house, and seen the poor wretches roasted in their armour like lobsters boiled in their shells . . . No, if I were training fighters for Outremer, I'd have them discard their armour, and go as light-armed as possible — naked if necessary."

"Oh, Madame!" The Abbot gave a horrified gasp. She took no notice but went on.

"Armed like the Greek peltasts of old, with bows and slings. I'd have them learn the shape of the land, the hidden ways and secret paths, and how to creep up on the enemy unawares."

"Like barbarians?" exclaimed the Sieur de Maltravers. "Unthinkable! Madame, don't you respect the dignity of war?"

"What's the dignity of war, if it's a question of winning the war?" she retorted. "If they want to win the war — I say, *if* they want to win it, which I sometimes doubt . . ."

Both the Abbot and the Sieur de Maltravers were eager to change the subject.

"Oh, look, Madame, here come the contestants."

The knights that were to take part in the tournament rode slowly past the grandstand, saluting as they went. There were twenty-four of them, a fine array of coloured silks, embroideries, banners, devices, all displayed upon their shining armour.

"Is the White Knight not among them?" inquired the Abbot. "I understood he was to ride today, and as a matter of fact I came especially to see him."

"Oh, he's to ride in the second part," said the Abbess. "He usually does that. By the Mass, I like the look of that young fellow in the middle rank — him in blue, with the white lion on the shield azure. Who is he, my Lord Maltravers?"

"That one? Oh, that's the young Sir Lioncel de Courcy, of Sherborne in Dorset. A promising young fellow. Younger son of a worthy house. He's ridden well in various places before now."

The Abbess's eyes dwelt with pleasure on the youngster: dark hair neatly cut in the Norman manner, well-marked brows above animated blue eyes, a short nose, full lips. He sat his horse well, and handled his lance easily.

"Oh, a good lad," the Sieur de Maltravers went on. "But the White Knight. Now, tell me more about him—"

"Oh, but Madame!" broke in the Abbot. "He's known all over the south country — 'as unknown and yet well known,' as the holy Apostle has it. He has never lost a jousting match yet. At every tourney he is there, and never fails to bear away the prize. Isn't that so, Madame?"

"Oh, yes," she agreed.

"He seems to be slightly built, as far as one can tell from his armour. For no one ever sees him out of it. He removes his helmet only for an instant to receive his crown and honour the Lady of the Tourney, and then those near enough to see — but no one sees him very near — say he seems like an old man with smooth white hair, thick white eyebrows, and a beard that hides his mouth. Yet, he does not move like an old man. Then he puts on his helmet again, and rides away no one knows where. Never speaks a word. None has ever heard his voice. Two men-servants wait on him, but they say no more than they must. Some simple folk think there's something unearthly about him." The Abbot gave a small deprecating smile. "But you and I, my Lord Maltravers, know what to make of such notions."

"He's a remarkable jouster, then?"

"Marvellous. And yet it's not by strength and weight, just by art and skill. He has a movement, a trick they say, that none is ever able to defeat. But you will see for yourselves. Ha! The first course is about to begin!"

With all the usual parade and formality, the first two contestants took their places — brilliant armour flashing in the sun, horses flouncing under their heavy draperies, the great cylindrical jousting helmets, with their monstrous erections of head-cloth, wreath, and crest making it impossible to recognise the men except by their colours and devices.

The two first contestants drew to the opposite ends of the field, each one on his own side of the barrière. Ceremoniously, a herald read the rules of combat. Then each knight lowered his lance, the sunlight flashing along the length of it, and fitted it into its "rest" on the saddle, balancing the butt end of it under his right arm. His left arm held his shield, bright with its blazon.

A trumpet blared, and they sprang toward each other, meeting with a shock and crash of metal across the barrière. One of them struck the other's shield fair and square, and the other went down. With practiced skill he fell clear of his horse, while his squires ran to pick him up; the victor sped on, amidst plaudits. So it went on — sometimes a man unhorsed, sometimes just a hit registered on the opponent's shield; and the winner, in each case, confronting the next in line until he himself was worsted.

Now it was Sir Lioncel's turn. The Abbess watched him with interest — she could know him by his colours, white on blue. She remembered his blue eyes. His blue-enamelled armour, with the great helm all in blue and white, made a brave show. His crest was the white lion, like the emblem on his blue shield.

With a fine, easy action he unhorsed his first opponent, and the crowd roared approval. Then the second. The Abbess followed his movements with technical interest. "He's good," she said to the Sieur de Maltravers, "but not good enough. He tires himself with unnecessary movements. I doubt he'll last the third course." Yet, he did. His opponent, a burly figure in red and yellow, went down before him. "That's better," said the Abbess. "That's three. That qualifies him to ride in the second part."

"I understand that that will be against the White Knight," said the Sieur de Maltravers.

"It might be," said the Abbess. "I'd like to see him match him. But he hasn't quite the skill. Look at that, now — ah!" For the next opponent, one in black and silver, caught the blue knight somehow off his guard, and he reeled and fell. The crowd gave a deep sigh of commiseration. "No matter," said the Abbess. "We'll see him ride again in the second part. If only he had a little more science!"

She lost interest now, and turned to chat with the two nuns behind her.

The Sieur de Maltravers wondered about the Abbess, as did many others. There was so much that people didn't know about her. It was known for certain, of course, that she ruled the immensely wealthy nunnery of Shaston, on the hill of Shaftesbury — the Convent and Order of Saint Evodias and Saint Syntyche — and that it had been bestowed on her, many years ago, by King Henry the Second (a kinsman of hers) as part of his penance for Becket; and that was — how many years ago? Then how old was she? Nobody quite knew. But it was known that like so many monastics of her time, she had set up her own Order and her own Rule, which was different in many ways from most Rules; but it was a perfectly legitimate Rule, having its charter from the Pope, who, everyone knew, was her cousin. Nor was he her only distinguished connection.

Maltravers was brought back from his musing. The first half of the tourney was over, and servants were bringing round wine and comfits. But the Abbess had risen from her seat.

"I fear I must leave you now, my Lord Maltravers and my Lord Abbot." She curtsied to each. "It is time for me to say my office."

"Oh, surely not so soon?" exclaimed Maltravers. "Are you not going to see the White Knight ride?"

"Alas, my lord, no. The first part has overrun its time a little, and I must not stay. Indeed I am sorry."

"Oh, but you did not see him last time, nor the time before," said the Abbot.

"Oh, I have seen him a time or two," she replied. "I should have liked to see young Lioncel ride against him, though. But, indeed, I must not stay.

Fare you well, my lords, and thank you for your company." With another low obeisance, she swept away, the two nuns following her, and was lost in the crowd below the stand.

The second part of the tournament was beginning.

"He's coming! The White Knight's coming!" The rumour ran around — along the courtly benches of the scarlet-draped stand, among the crowd on the grass below. Heads were turned, necks were craned. He came riding in at the far end — a slim figure even in all that armour, on a white Arab horse — his armour, and the drapery of his helmet, his shield and all about him, pure white. There was no crest above his helmet, and no device on his shield; but here and there decorations of silver and crystal caught the light.

"The White Knight! The White Knight!" the crowd yelled to its hero. Some on the grandstand cried *Vive le Blanc!* for as much French as English was spoken there.

Unable to turn his head because of the great cylindrical helmet almost as wide as his shoulders, the White Knight acknowledged the cheers of the crowd, and the patronage of the Sieur de Maltravers, with a wave of his hand in its silvery gauntlet.

"Isn't he magnificent?" said a pretty young lady who had slipped into the place vacated by the Abbess to the right of the Sieur de Maltravers. She was his daughter, and very charming she looked, all in gold tissue, with a tall steeple-shaped "hennin," from which a filmy white veil floated. "Oh, I'm sure he'll defeat all comers. But I'd like to see the Blue Knight unhorse him all the same."

"The Blue . . . oh, young De Courcy," rejoined her father, with a smile, and a lift of his eyebrows. "To be sure. Well, we shall see what we shall see. Have you made a wager on him then?"

"Er — not exactly," she said, letting the white veil float over her reddening cheeks.

The other combatants were entering now — a rainbow of colours, each colour with its blazon and its crest. These were the picked men, who had each stayed more than three courses. As the Blue Knight came by, the Sieur de Maltravers thought he could see something golden attached to the blue head-piece. It looked like a woman's glove.

As before, the combatants were paired by lot, and each who defeated his opponent took on the next on the list, and so on till he himself was unhorsed. Young Lioncel's turn came when the man before him had beaten three opponents.

The Sieur de Maltravers leaned toward his daughter.

"The Abbess ought to be here to see this, Marguerite."

His daughter hardly answered him. Her attention was all on the Blue Knight.

Gallop, jingle — crash! With a sufficiently neat movement, the Blue Knight scored on his opponent's shield. Marguerite clapped her hands and jumped up and down in her seat. So the second, the third, and fourth he unhorsed. The fifth was the White Knight. The crowd watched breathlessly. Marguerite's face went from red to pale.

The glittering figures, white and blue, hurtled toward each other — Crash! and the Blue Knight was rolling on the ground. It had all happened too quickly for Marguerite to see how it had been. Some cunning stroke, some skillful movement . . .

The crowd shouted for the victor, though there were some commiserating groans for young Lioncel. Marguerite sank back and put her veil to her eyes.

"The White Knight's Gambit," said Maltravers. "That's what they call it. It never fails, and no one can find out how he does it. Are you all right, my dear?"

"Oh, yes," she replied, rallying herself. "I . . . yes, I had put a wager on him. It's no matter."

The White Knight went on to defeat opponent after opponent, remaining, at the end, victor over all comers. Finally, he rode up to the dais, and removed his great helm. Marguerite placed the crown upon his head, but all she could see of him was an abundant poll of white hair, crisply curling, white eyebrows so bushy they almost hid the eyes, a white beard, close-cut but thick, that hid most of his face. He spoke no word, but made all the gestures of courtesy, while the trumpets acclaimed him . . . and so rode away.

Young Lioncel was sitting disconsolate in his pavilion, while his squire, having removed his armour, dressed his scratches and abrasions, and massaged his bruised shoulder. A light tap sounded on the shield that hung outside. The squire went out, and returned.

"Two nuns, sir," he said. "They insist on seeing you."

"Oh, God . . . Give them two gold pieces and send them away."

"Your pardon, sir, but they say they don't want money. They say they have a message. For your ears only."

"Oh?" A sudden flicker of hope. Could it be from Marguerite after all? "Let them come in, Simon, and leave us. Oh, give me my robe first, for heaven's sake."

He turned and rose, rather stiffly, as the nuns came in. But their first words disappointed him.

"We are from the Abbess of Shaston." (Fool that he was, to expect a message from Marguerite, even though he had worn her gage.) "We are to say this: If you would learn how to defeat the White Knight, come to the Convent of Saint Evodias and Saint Syntyche, at Shaston, and she herself will tell you of one who will teach you what to do."

Not Marguerite, but perhaps . . . ?

"Tell the Reverend Mother," he said, "that I will come."

They curtsied, blessed him, and went away without another word.

The Abbess's parlour was a place of restrained elegance. No grille — the nuns lived (when at home) behind a grille, not so much to keep them in as to keep intruders out; but the Abbess received her guests without any such apparatus. A charming solar chamber, hung with light-coloured hangings embroidered with the most cheerful of saints and angels; large pots of flowers everywhere (for it was summer), an embroidery frame, and a chess table. She made him welcome with excellent Cyprus wine in silver cups. Sitting at ease by her embroidery frame, she contemplated him.

"I'd like to help you," she said. "I'm a critic of jousting, and I know you've the stuff of champions in you, but you need more science."

He could but agree, watching her shapely hands as she moved the embroidery frame aside and turned to the chessboard.

"Let me show you," she said. She proceeded to set upon the board no ordinary chessmen, but two knights, modelled in silver, much larger than the usual chessmen; and these were not the conventional horse-headed shapes, but the whole figure of the knight and his horse, complete in every detail. He cried out in wonder at the beauty of them. She handed one of them to him, and showed him how both arms were articulated, at the shoulder, the elbow, and the wrist, so that every kind of movement could be simulated.

"Oh, but these are marvellous!" he exclaimed. "They're not of this world. Did the elves make them for you?"

"Not quite," she said, smiling. "A Saracen made them in the Holy Land. But that's another story. Now, we'll place them on the board, and I'll show you."

So she demonstrated to him, clearly and with patience, the ordinary movements of jousting, and the logic and reason for them, and how they could be refined and improved, and how each move could be countered by another. He was completely fascinated. An hour went by unnoticed.

"Now," she said, "the bells will ring soon and you must go. But if you would like me to teach you, you must prepare to stay in Shaston for some days, or even some weeks. There is a guesthouse in the town. Tomorrow at matins, you must be in the meadow at the foot of Shaston Hill, with your horse and your armour, and a certain knight will come and practice all this with you. He will not speak to you, for he's under a vow. But he'll show you plainly enough. I shall be watching you, though you won't see me. Tomorrow you will come here again, and I will tell you how you did. And so on, the next day and the next. Will you do this?"

"Oh, Madame!" He was enraptured.

"Be sure and have your great jousting helmet," she said, "and stuff it well with straw. You'll take a tumble or two."

He was punctual at his appointment, just as the bell for matins was ringing. The place was easy to find, a smooth expanse of green among the apple orchards at the foot of the long hillroad that winds down from Shaftesbury. He looked up toward the convent, but it was well out of sight. He looked round for any house, or hut, or building from which the Abbess could watch him unseen, but there was none. Hardly a hedge or a coppice, yet she had said she would see him, and afterward criticise his performance. Then, how . . . ? Strange things were whispered about that lady, the Abbess. He began to remember some of them, and his hair stirred a little on his head. But no time for thought — here came his instructor. Not a very large man, nor in very bright armour. In fact, his armour was very plain and rather battered, and all of a dull bronze colour, like leather, without any decoration, blazon, crest or other adornment, but well-kept for a practice suit. The helmet hid the face completely, and as Lioncel had been warned, the man did not speak, but by gestures he made his instructions quite plain.

A row of hurdles had been laid down the middle of the meadow for a barriére, and along it, at points where they might be needed, quantities of straw. The instructor handed Lioncel a spear with a padded point. Then they began their practice.

They rode course after course, and at first Lioncel found himself unable to connect with his opponent at all, missing his shield and just running past him.

Or he received the other's padded spear full on his shield, sometimes tumbling back over his horse's crupper. He had long ago learnt the art of falling safely. But at the end of an hour's practice he found himself bruised and battered, and glad enough to stop. The unknown held up his hand, bowed a little with his helmeted head, and cantered away round the turn of the hill. Lioncel rode slowly back to his lodgings in the town, wincing and groaning.

The Abbess received him with smiles the next morning, and commiserated with him on his bruises, offering him a jar of herbal ointment which he gratefully accepted. She then produced the two silver knights, and systematically analysed where he had gone wrong. But how, he pondered again, how on earth had she seen him? And again he reflected on the uncanny things he had heard about her.

He considered her, indeed, very thoughtfully, over the three weeks that his course of lessons lasted. He could not fail to notice how fine and expressive her great dark-brown eyes were, and how noble the proportions of her brow. Her skin was smooth, her lips red, her teeth perfect. How old was she? Nobody knew. Sometimes she seemed young. Then, again, from the things she remembered, and from the way she spoke, she must have been much older than she appeared. There was a warm and welcoming charm about her. They talked of a great many things besides jousting, and Lioncel found himself confiding in her, almost as if she were his mother. Indeed, he had a mother living, but she was a proud, formal lady, who had left most of his upbringing to nurses. One could not tell her anything. Certainly there was a need in his life that this gentle nun, in her soft white draperies, had begun to fill.

And all this while he had not been to Stanton Maltravers, and Marguerite was beginning to wonder why.

At the end of the second week the Abbess showed him, with the silver knights, exactly how the White Knight's Gambit was done. He was a quick learner, and the next day, when he faced his instructor in the meadow, he tried it out — and made it work. The brown knight tumbled over his horse's crupper, and rolled on the straw. Frightened at what he had done, Lioncel leapt from his horse and ran to help him; but the brown knight was on his feet without assistance, and quickly in the saddle again. Lioncel thought that he could hear a strange noise in the depth of that great beehive of a helmet — something like laughter. The brown knight, by unmistakable gestures, signified that he should continue. They spent the rest of the hour perfecting the stroke, but without either actually unhorsing the other. When the brown knight saluted and rode away, Lioncel again thought he heard a sort of deep chuckle smothered in the helmet.

The Abbess knew all about this, too — and congratulated him, smiling. They spent another six days, theory and practice, turn and turn about, and then the Abbess pronounced him ready to go and take on all challengers. There was no need to swear him to secrecy as to the mysterious White Knight's Gambit, for it was a thing that could not be imparted to another save by personal demonstration; but she asked him, and he agreed very willingly, to keep the secret of where he had learnt it.

So now there began to be something new in the jousting world. The young Sir Lioncel de Courcy of Sherborne suddenly emerged as a star of the first brilliance. He was victorious over all comers, beginning to eclipse the fame of the White Knight, who was now not so often seen. The Blue Knight was the favorite. He won at Canterbury and Rochester, at Dover and at Sandwich. Then at Hastings and Pevensey, at Winchester and Corfe, at Dorchester and Exeter. Everywhere men heard his name. And he was seen again at Stanton Maltravers.

"I have been taking lessons," he told Marguerite. "But I am forbidden to tell you who taught me."

And with that she had to be content. But, indeed, she was more than content, for she crowned him the victor again and again, and her golden glove still nestled among his blue helm-draperies. The other golden glove disappeared from her bower about that time, and she knew that he slept with it under his pillow.

But so far he had not encountered the White Knight — until the day when he came to ride at Christchurch in Hampshire.

This, he felt, was the moment for which he had been preparing. He would have liked to tell the Abbess about it, but she, it seemed, was in the Holy Land once more. But he told Marguerite, and indeed she journeyed with her father from Stanton Maltravers to be present.

So this is it, he said to himself, as he went over his equipment with Simon, his squire, and personally helped him to groom his fine bay horse. There he was mounted and away, with Marguerite and her father watching him. And there his opponent was, the glittering White Knight, so like one of the Abbess's silver knights.

The trumpet sounded, away he went –– gallop, gallop –– remember what she taught you; yes, this is the way –– crash!

And nobody was more surprised than he himself to see the crystal and silver image fall as he smote it, and roll on the ground, while he swept on, and the crowd roared. He had done it; he had conquered the White Knight.

As he knelt, bareheaded, to receive the crown from Marguerite, the White Knight was close beside him, clasping his hand, laying a fraternal arm across his shoulder. For just a minute he saw him unhelmed, glimpsed the smooth white hair, ruffled into curls by the helmet, and the eyes, kindly and admiring, looking out from the bush of face-hair like a sheepdog's. Then he was gone. Lioncel was on top of the world.

He gave her a long and full account of how he had conquered the White Knight, a "blow by blow" description, with all the technicalities. He laid out the two silver knights on the chessboard, and when he had shown the defeat of his adversary, he took the one that represented the White Knight, drew the man from the horse, rolled it on the chessboard as if on the ground, and picking up a quill pen, thrashed the little figure's backside with it. The Abbess's face reddened, and she drew her brows together.

"You forget your knightly courtesy," she said.

"Oh, I'm sorry," he said, hanging his head like a naughty child. Carefully he put the silver man back on its horse. Then he went on and told the Abbess of the final tournament at Sarum, of the Queen's visit, and of the prize for that tournament. "My heart's desire at last, dear lady," he said — not noticing how she had changed colour again, and was now very pale and biting her lips.

"Wish me success, dear godmother," he said.

"Wish you — ? Oh, of course. Yes, to be sure. God bless you," and absently she traced a cross over him.

"Will you not come and see me ride, then?"

"I? No, I think not — I — maybe I'm getting too old to care for such things."

"Too old?" he exclaimed. "Never in the world! Dear lady, you never grow older." But he could not understand the bitterness in her voice.

The great day had come. There was the Queen herself, in her rich robes, with her crown of gold and pearls above the softly draped wimple; the Sieur de Maltravers, beaming and expansive in scarlet and miniver; and Marguerite beside him, in a dress of lighter blue than her knight's, the colour of an early summer morning sky, and with a chaplet of flowers in her hair — almost a bridal array. Lioncel's heart seemed to turn over at the sight of her. Two nuns of the Shaston order sat behind her, as representing the Abbess; but of the Abbess herself there was no sign.

The tournament began with all the due formalities, which were long and comprehensive. Finally, the Sieur de Maltravers, sitting by the side of Queen Eleanor herself, stood up and read from a scroll a declaration that the prize of the tourney, by the special request of her Grace the Queen, should be the hand in marriage of his youngest daughter, the Lady Marguerite. He called all those present to witness this promise, attested by a sacred oath, and agreed to by all the combatants. And Lioncel felt a cold sweat break out all over him, and did not dare to look up at Marguerite.

It was all very well arranged: twelve contests only, and Lioncel's name third from the end, so that however long the other combatants stayed the course, he would not have more than three to face, and could reasonably be expected to beat the last of those.

All began according to plan. A pretty good rider had come to the point where Lioncel should meet him — a formidable knight it was, with a red shield and the device of a harp. This man had scored against three, not unhorsing them, but hitting their shields squarely in the centre. Lioncel took the red shield strongly and accurately in the middle of the device, making it ring like a gong. He galloped on along the barriére, turned at the end, and awaited the next opponent.

Then there was a stir and a delay. The crowd at the other end of the field parted, and in rode the White Knight himself.

There was anxious conferring, among the Marshal, the Sieur de Maltravers, and the Queen. The crowd had seen the White Knight arrive, and acclaimed him noisily. So, after much agitated consultation, the Marshal blew a trumpet, waited till there was silence, and proclaimed:

"Your Grace the Queen — my lords, ladies and gentles all, and all you good people here — I proclaim that we have with us today, by unexpected good fortune, the famous and glorious White Knight, hitherto champion of all the southern lands of England, and conquered by none but the honoured Sir Lioncel here before you. It is therefore agreed that my lord the White Knight shall ride the thirteenth course, against Sir Lioncel or whoever may have succeeded him, and that the prize shall be, as before stated, the hand of the fair Lady Marguerite . . . God Save King Richard!"

And the crowd cheered, but Lioncel held tight to his wits, to keep the world from spinning around him. He forced himself to concentrate hard on the technique he would need to use, and tried not to let the trembling of his body communicate itself to the horse beneath him.

Away again. Another hit, easy. And another one, a yellow armour this time, well and truly unhorsed. And now — now for the White Knight. He had the famous "gambit" clear in his mind and muscles, as he had worked it before . . . now for it. But what went wrong? He felt the stunning crash, the slipping and falling. He was on the ground, almost too stunned to know when the attendants dragged him out of danger and helped him to his feet.

He struggled out of his helmet in time to hear the Marshal proclaiming:

"I therefore declare the winner of this tourney is the noble lord, the White Knight, and to him is awarded the hand in marriage of the beautiful and noble Lady Marguerite."

Lioncel groped around for his squire's arm.

"Get me away from here. Get me to the tent. Yes, tell them I'm wounded — anything." And he staggered out blindly, the young squire supporting him, leaving behind the acclaim of the crowd, nobles and commoners alike, for the White Knight.

And up on the grandstand, regardless of the Queen's presence, Marguerite was sitting with her head in her hands, weeping bitterly.

Inside his pavilion, Lioncel sank down on his couch and started throwing his armour off as the squire unlaced it.

"The end of everything," he said. "Take these things away, Simon. I shan't want them any more. All I want now is a rope. It must be a silken rope. Simon, go out and get me a silken rope, quickly. It must be a silken rope, for the honour of knighthood. Bring it to that great barn behind the stables. Hurry, Simon, hurry!"

"Yes, my lord," said Simon, puzzled but not questioning, and ran out.

A silken rope? But what for? And how to find one? The boy ran on, with but the one idea in his mind. There were two nuns standing waiting below the grandstand. They had blue girdles, made of silken cord. He looked no farther. He had been told to hurry.

"Lady," he said breathlessly to one of them, "Can you lend me your girdle? My lord Sir Lioncel sent me for a silken rope."

"A silken rope?" she said, frowning. "But what on earth for?"

"I don't know, lady. He said for the honour of knighthood."

A startled exclamation made him look up. He had not noticed that the White Knight himself was sitting on his horse close above him, with his helm discarded. The astonished squire was the first to hear the mysterious white-bearded man speak, but in a strange voice, not what one would expect of an old man.

"Oh, good God — they *hang* knights with silken ropes! For God's sake, where is he?"

"Over at the barn," the squire faltered.

Without a word more, the White Knight, still mounted, spurred his horse and galloped clean through the crowd that parted in terror to let him by. Straight in a breakneck rush for the barn.

Lioncel had not waited for Simon. He had found a silken cord in the bed-hangings of his tent; and he was now sitting on his restless, nervous horse, tying an end of the cord to a rafter in the barn, and fitting the other end round his neck.

The White Knight, with Simon panting on foot behind him, sprang from his horse and entered the barn. One look was enough.

"Oh, you fool. Oh, you unspeakable fool!" the White Knight exclaimed. "Put that rope down. You, squire, hold his horse. Oh, you fool, you fool — listen to me!"

The voice was astonishing, but Lioncel had heard it before. Dropping the rope and leaving it to dangle from the rafter, he watched paralysed with amazement, as the White Knight's fingers stripped off the thick white hair, the bushy eyebrows, the beard and all.

"Do you know me now, my son?" said the Abbess.

Later, in the privacy of his pavilion, when his amazement had somewhat subsided, she told him:

"God knows I never meant it to go as far as that. Oh, may the Lord forgive me, boy, I was jealous. It was a little blow to my pride when you unhorsed me — although I had taught you how to do it — but when I knew you would use my skill to win *her*. Oh, forgive me, boy. It's ridiculous of me — old enough to — oh, never mind."

His eyes filled with tears.

"Oh, lady, I never knew . . ."

"Of course you never knew," she said, a trifle gruffly, and buried her face in a handkerchief. "Here, let's not have a high romantic scene, that our good Queen Eleanor would delight in. You're young, and I'm . . . not so young. I suppose it was as much pride as anything else. Come now, send your squire for the Sieur de Maltravers. Have him come here as privily as possible. As for the Queen, I'll tell her later on. I know her well."

Outside, the crowd waited, full of rumours and excited surmises. But Marguerite was not crying now, for a nun had whispered to her something she had heard from a squire.

And long before the hour was out, the Marshal had blown his trumpet again, and said (after all the proper flourishes):

"Let it be known that the high and mighty and victorious White Knight has disclosed to the noble Sieur de Maltravers and to Her Grace the Queen, that there is a reason by which he is disqualified from winning this tourney, and the prize therefore goes by right to the noble and excellent Sir Lioncel de Courcy of Serborne in Dorset – God save King Richard!"

The rest was drowned in the acclamations as Marguerite set the crown upon the head of Lioncel, and he set his ring upon her finger.

But the White Knight could nowhere be seen.

III.
THE
JUSTICE
OF THE
ABBESS _____

"Are you trying to tell me, Madame," said Guido D'Este, Sub-Prior of the Order of St John of Jerusalem, "that Galen and Avicenna were fools?"

The Sub-Prior's fine Italian countenance was cold with scorn. In his rich black robe, emblazoned with the square-ended white crosses, he faced the Abbess of Shaston in her snowy white; between them lay a sick man on his bed.

"Water," moaned the man.

"Why, no," the Abbess replied to the Sub-Prior, smiling without pride. "Not at all. Galen and Avicenna were wise men, who observed and recorded, but they did *not* blindly follow what someone else had laid down in other cases. They noticed what was in front of their eyes. And in this present case I am sure they would either of them have given drink, and plenty of it, to this poor man, and not have bled him."

"Water, for God's sake," the sick man sighed.

"Madame," said the Sub-Prior, frowning portentously, "both Galen and Avicenna teach us in their books that a man in fever must on no account be given drink, for it is only the fever that craves what will excite it. And as for bleeding, it has always been done and always will be."

"Yes, and so the patients will always die," she retorted. "Because in some cases, not always like this, blessed Galen found it better to withhold fluids. But this poor man, his vital spirits are all burnt up, and anyone can see he needs drink. You've bled him till he hasn't enough blood in his body to feed a flea, and God knows he needs all the fluid he can get to make up the loss. Yes, of course you can cool a fevered body by bleeding it — until you cool it to death. My lord, I mean no disrespect, but I beseech you to let me treat this man as I think best. He will certainly die otherwise."

A strange expression crossed Guido D'Este's face, but he smoothed it away, and turned, shrugging his black-draped shoulders.

"Oh, on your conscience be it then. A dying man — his final dispatching be your guilt. Have it as you please." He shouldered his way out of the narrow cell.

The Abbess wasted no time. She turned to the young novice who had been waiting behind her.

"Quick now, Brother Richard," she said. "Get a large pitcher of cool spring water, with citron juice and hydromel and just a little salt. By the grace of God we'll save this man yet. Oh, and a silver cup and spoon."

The sick man's eyes focussed uncertainly upon the hand that lifted a spoonful of the heavenly liquid to his lips.

"Angel," he said. "Angel . . ."

When after some hours the Sub-Prior came by on his rounds again, the sick man was relaxed and sleeping quietly, with his brow moist and sweating. The Abbess sat by his side sponging his face. The Sub-Prior raised his eyebrows, but said nothing.

Later, the sick man woke, weak and exhausted, but in his right mind, with the fever gone.

"You have saved me," he said to the Abbess, and included in his words young Brother Richard. "I feel I shall recover now. You came, as Lazarus was not allowed to do for Dives, and cooled my tongue in the flame. I owe my life to you. Yes, and to you, Brother."

Later he asked the Abbess to write to his wife for him. "She is in Constantinople," he said. "The Lady Anna des Aigues-Mortes." He drew himself up on his pillows as best he could. "I am the Sieur des Aigues-Mortes at your service, Reverend Lady," and he did his best to bow toward her. "Of the Langue of Provence, but my wife is an Armenian lady. She is well known in Constantinople. Tell her that I was sick of a fever, but I am now recovering, and hope to return soon. And that I love her dearly."

The noble Hospital of St John of Jerusalem was a vast hall, one storey up, and reached by a wide staircase, lit by windows far up in the walls, vaulted over like a church — at one end a large fireplace, where in the short but frosty winter a good fire could keep the cold and the damp out; at the other end an altar where every day Mass was said, so that the patients could have the comfort of the Presence of God. All round the walls, little cells, just big enough for a sick man's bed, with two entrances, so that he could be carried in and carried out by the serving brothers. Room for other beds to be laid out along the wide hall, while the serious cases were treated in the cells; but it was not often, except after a battle or during a plague, that so many beds were needed. With curtains of wool and linen, the place could be made comfortable enough, according to the standards of the time; and what the Brothers, both professed and lay, fell short of in medical knowledge, they made up in affectionate care and devotion.

The position of the Abbess of Shaston was certainly not in accordance with the rules. When she presented herself to the Grand Master, and demanded to be allowed to nurse the sick and wounded, at first the Brothers were for shutting the door in her face. Such a thing could not possibly be allowed. But the Prior was a good friend of hers, a kinsman also, so she persevered, and made a convincing case to the Grand Master himself. And somehow, she was a woman to whom it was very hard to say "no." As the Grand Master found. And so here she was, nobody quite knew on what footing, answerable only to the

Superior, who directed the actual work of the Hospital, and apparently on an equality with the physicians — or at least she seemed to think so.

The fact was, they needed helpers very badly at that moment. Small but lethal skirmishes round Jerusalem, and the diseases attendant upon hot weather, had filled them up with casualties. They could not afford to turn down any offers of help. But the Grand Master would admit only the Abbess herself, not the escort of two Sisters that custom demanded. One female was enough. Three would be an invasion.

"But, Madame, you need have no fear for your safety or your reputation," he insisted. "We are all men under vows here, and you yourself a lady in religion, also under a vow. Also, if I may say so, no longer young . . ."

But he questioned within himself. *Was* she no longer young? His eyes searched the smooth face discreetly framed by the white wimple and gorget. How old was she really? That was one of the things that nobody knew, one of the many questions about her.

So here she was, as dusk fell, going along the upper storey cloister that adjoined the great hall, toward her little bare cell at the corner of the quadrangle. Young Brother Richard carried a torch to light her.

"Good night, my good Brother," she said to him with affection, as she took the torch from him.

"Thank you for your help. You've done a good day's work today. Are you tired?"

"A little, Madame," he admitted. "But I'm so happy to have done what we did for that poor man. He will recover now, won't he?"

"Yes, with God's help," she said. "Now, are you sure you can manage this watch, until Brother Peter relieves you at midnight?"

"Why, yes indeed, Madame." His eyes glowed up at her. His face was pale, but his zeal shone out of him. "It's nothing. But you, Madame, you must rest. You watched with him all last night."

"Yes, I'll admit I can do with some sleep now." She stifled a yawn. "A peaceful watch to you, then, in God's name." She restrained her impulse to place a motherly kiss on his forehead.

The Abbess knew that Brother Richard — not known by his family name any longer — was an orphan of good family in England. There were all too many orphans of good families in Outremer. And he was only seventeen. Many years yet, before he could become a Knight Hospitaller, but that was what he had set himself to become. She sighed as she thought of his youth, his fresh beauty, his idealism. Please God that nothing may spoil it, she prayed.

She had been deeply asleep for a long time, she thought, when she was jerked awake. Someone was raining blows on her door, and shouting.

"Madame! Madame! Madame! Oh, for God's sake . . ."

She recognised young Brother Richard's voice.

"I'm coming. Wait. Wait."

She slipped on her habit and girt it round her, and her cloak, pulling the hood up, not waiting to adjust wimple, gorget, and veil. Barefooted, she hurried to the door and opened it.

In the dim light the boy's face was livid.

"Oh, Madame — the Sieur des Aigues-Mortes — he's dead!"

"What? He couldn't be! He was out of danger."

"Not the fever, Madame. Killed! Killed in his sleep. With a knife."

They stood in the little alcove, looking down at the body of the Sieur des Aigues-Mortes. The blood had soaked his bedsheets and was dripping to the floor — the last drops from the deep wound, squarely in the heart. The weapon still stood there.

Brother Richard's teeth were chattering. "I fell asleep," he managed to articulate. "I did, I fell asleep. My fault, my grievous fault. I knew nothing. I woke, and saw . . . this!"

The sound had alerted others of the Hospitallers and the lay-brothers. Suddenly there was a ring of silent faces looking over the shoulders of Brother Richard and the Abbess. The pale stern face of the Sub-Prior, with his black brows and beard, loomed over Brother Richard.

"Who has done this damnable thing?" his deep voice boomed. No one moved, except Brother Richard, who fell on his knees by the body, covering his face with his hands, shaking with suppressed sobs.

"Whose dagger is this?" said the Sub-Prior, his voice soft with menace.

Every man's hand went to the right side of his belt, where each one carried his dagger, a thing necessary for many peaceful uses. On the left side of the belt was the place for the sword, which a professed Knight Hospitaller would wear in battle.

"Whose dagger is missing?" asked the Sub-Prior. Brother Richard lifted his head, stood up, put his hand to his dagger-sheath.

"Oh God!" he cried. "Gone. Stolen . . ."

The Sub-Prior stooped and drew the dagger out from the wound. A belated gush of blood followed it. A deep sighing gasp came from the crowd. A murdered man's corpse bleeds afresh in the presence of the murderer, it was said.

"Is this yours?" the Sub-Prior asked Brother Richard.

"Yes, it's mine. Oh, God help me! I didn't kill him. Oh, as God's my witness, I didn't kill him. How could I? He was a good man."

The boy stood looking this way and that, from face to face in the dimness. He seemed dazed, stupefied. The Sub-Prior's hand descended heavily on his shoulder.

"Come," he said.

At the touch, the boy's control broke. He shrieked aloud, the sound echoing explosively in the stone arches, a wild wordless cry. Then:

"Oh no! Oh no! I didn't do it, Father. Can't you believe me? Oh God! Oh God!"

"Take him away," said the Sub-Prior.

It was impossible, of course, that the Abbess should be admitted into the Chapter-House for the trial. Brother Richard was tried by the assembled Council of the Order of St John. Only the high officers among the professed Knights could enter there. The Abbess stood at the massive arched entrance, and waited. Tall and white-robed, and very still, she did not at all look like a suppliant waiting at the gate — much more like a vigilant angel.

After long deliberation — she had watched the shadows creep a long way round — there was a stir, the doors opened, and the accused boy, firmly held by two tall impassive Knights, was led past her and away. He saw her there, and turned on her red-rimmed eyes full of terror and supplication.

The Knights in their black robes filed out two by two, the Grand Master having departed by his own private entrance. She scanned the faces. They were grim.

The Prior, her friend and kinsman, came by. She stepped up to him.

"How did it go?"

"Why, of course, they consider him guilty. All the evidence shows it. But he denies it."

"So — ?"

"So he is to take the ordeal by fire. He himself has accepted it. That should settle the matter once for all. Oh, I'm sorry, my Lady Abbess. I know you liked the lad, and worked with him. He seemed a good lad, but who knows the heart of man?"

"Who indeed?" she said. "But what motive had he?"

"Motive? What need of motive when the Evil One enters a man's soul? The Devil overrides all motives."

"Then," she said, "the boy must be mad, and not responsible for his actions."

"Not so, Lady. Otherwise, no sinner would be responsible for his actions. This is the Adversary's work, and must be fought accordingly."

She signed, half turning away. "What is to be the form of the ordeal?"

"He is to walk over red-hot coals of fire, two hundred clothyards, before all of us. If he survives, and his feet show no blisters after three days, he is innocent. If not, the law must take its course. I still think he should have confessed his guilt, so that he could die shriven. For if the fire overcomes him, he could die in his sin."

The Abbess drew her white veil over her face, so that he could not see her shuddering.

She visited the prisoner in his cell. It was the usual dark, foul place, deep under the building. He sat, wrapped in his black mantle, the cowl drawn over his face, looking like nothing but a black stump in the darkness. But he roused himself, as she came in. She put out her arms and held him to keep him from falling on the ground at her feet, and did not shrink from the foulness of his mantle. A guard followed her, holding a taper.

"Give me that taper," she said to the guard, "and now go, and do not listen outside."

And such was the force of her command that he obeyed her, although it was against his orders.

At first the boy's words were incoherent; then he said, "I did not kill him. Oh, Madame, I did not kill him."

"I know you did not," she said. "I know you are innocent."

"What reason should I have to kill him? He was a good man, and kind to me. And yet I am not quite guiltless. I slept at my post, and allowed this dreadful thing to happen. In this I am guilty."

"But not of murder! Oh, there's a difference. I know you could never, never have murder in your heart. Do you believe that the fire will spare you because you are innocent?"

She could feel, in the dimness, how he turned his head aside.

"No, Madame," he said in a shaking voice. "I don't. The fire is fire, and will do its work on me."

Her voice was very tender.

"Don't you believe in God, Brother Richard?"

"Oh, yes – God forgive me, of course I believe in God. But I don't think I believe in the ordeal. How do they *know* that God will answer by a miracle? Listen, Madame. There was a woman in the village where I lived – a good honest girl – who was accused of stealing the silver chalice out of the church. They put her to the ordeal for theft. She had to take hold of a bar of white-hot iron . . . I saw it done. It shrivelled her hand to the white bones. They judged her guilty, and her hand should have been cut off. But before it was done, she died of the pain. Then, long afterward, it was found that the secton was the thief. They pronounced her innocent then. But the poor maid was dead." His voice vanished in sobs for a moment. "So you see, Madame, I am afraid of the fire."

She pressed both his hands firmly. They were hot, dry, and shaking.

"My child," she said, "I will save you if I can, God helping me. If you do not trust God, at least trust me!" (But this is all wrong, she said within herself. He should believe in God, not in me. Still, perhaps if he *begins* by believing in me – ?)

"Now," she said, "look up, and look at me."

Releasing his desperate grasp, she took the taper, which she had placed, when she came in, on a ledge of the rocky wall, and moved it so that the light would fall full on her face.

"Look at me. Throw back your cowl, stand up-right, and look me right in the eyes. So. Like that. Now, when you come to the ordeal, you will see me right before you, across the fire. Look right at me — right into my eyes as you are doing now. Nothing else. Look at me then as you are looking now, and look nowhere else. You will be safe."

Then she traced a cross on his forehead, picked up the taper, and called to the man outside. Without giving the taper back to him, she went slowly up the dark stairs.

Men had worked all night making the fire in the courtyard. Wood, charcoal, all manner of combustibles — a long bed of fire was being built up in a rectangular pit, two hundred clothyards long, and ten clothyards wide. It lay along the north side of the central quadrangle of the Hospital, in a line with the great staircase. This was built flush against the north wall of the quadrangle, a noble staircase of stone leading up to the level of the great hall — ten clothyards wide at least, so that the Knights Hospitallers and the serving Brethren could carry up their patients on stretchers — and sometimes carry them down again. It had no balustrade against its outer side, for the Hospitallers needed no such thing.

Now, seats were arranged on the steps of this staircase for the Great Officers and their guests, among whom was the Abbess. A strong barrier divided off two thirds of the quadrangle, where the public were to be admitted to see the ordeal. They had waited for many hours, and as soon as the sun rose they were admitted.

The Officers took their places. On the lowest step was a row of men-at-arms, and next a row of novice knights. Nobody envied them their position, for where they sat they could feel the heat of the fire. Then came the seat of the Grand Master, awesome in his black mantle, and his cap with the square-ended white cross. On his right was the Prior, and on his left the Abbess, with two nuns attendant on her in the row behind. In that row, also, over the Abbess's left shoulder, was Guido D'Este. All of them being seated and looking forward over the bed of fire, they did not look at each other's faces.

The fire below was now a smokeless, flickering red carpet. Its heat came up like the breath of a furnace, and the air quivered above it. Over its surface was a dusting of grey ash, like a crust. Where this broke, the intense red below showed through.

All rose to their feet as the Grand Master, in his deep and awesome voice, uttered prayers; he sprinkled holy water on the fire. It met the fire with a venomous hiss.

Then the Grand Master bade those on the steps be seated, and keep calm minds, and pray for God's justice. And the crowd pressed hard against the barrier, craning their necks to see the victim enter.

He came, guarded by two Knights. He was wrapped in his black habit, but they stripped it off him, so that he stood naked except for a white loincloth. A beautiful boy in the tenderness of his youth.

He stood, searching the faces before him, and his eyes met those of the Abbess. Met, and were fixed. Like one in a dream, he kept his gaze, eyes to eyes. And as the knights urged him forward, he moved like a sleepwalker. He stretched out his hands before him. The men placed him at the edge of the fiery pit, and released him. He set his foot upon the fire.

A deep "Ah . . ." went up from the crowd.

His face never changed, as he brought the other foot forward, never looking down, but always straight before him. Step by step by step — not hurrying, not flinching, not seeming to feel anything, or see anything but those eyes that held his. The Abbess breathed deeply, never once shifting her gaze — putting forth all her power — and who knows what powers beyond her own?

He came on steadily. Even the Grand Master watched in wonder. There seemed to be all round the boy, from head to feet, a kind of sheath of cool pearly white. And, then, outside of that, there sprang out all round him an aura of flames and flashes — red and green and yellow, all the fiery colours, surrounding him with blazing light where he walked unharmed.

He reached the foot of the steps, walking straight as his outstretched arms pointed, toward the Abbess. Then he swerved a little to the left of her, and the terrified men-at-arms and novices made way for him, as the flaming figure, still spellbound, ascended the steps and walked straight toward Guido D'Este — pointing now with his right hand straight to the Sub-Prior's breast.

A strange voice, not his own, came from the advancing figure.

"That man," it said. "Search him there."

And at that the Sub-Prior gave a great cry that was heard by all the terrified crowd. As the fiery forefinger touched him, he turned about and rushed up the stone stairs, all making way before him. Up to the top, high above the courtyard — to the unfenced edge — and down, crashing to sudden death upon the stones.

From every side men rushed to where the Sub-Prior had fallen. The Abbess detained two serving-men. The boy was standing dazed by her side, all sign of fire gone from him.

"Throw water over him," she said, "and tend him well till I come and see him," and she ran down to where the dead man was lying.

In his bosom, where Brother Richard had pointed, they found a letter. The superscription made it clear that it came from the Lady Anna des Aigues-Mortes, in Constantinople — the wife of the murdered man. But it was written in the Cyrillic script.

"None here can read it," said the Grand Master.

"But I can," said the Abbess. "Give it to me." She looked at it, frowned, and sighed.

"Read it," said the Grand Master.

"Not here, Most Puissant," she said. "To you alone, and in private."

So they carried away the body of the Sub-Prior, in deep sadness, and the Abbess and the Grand Master walked slowly away together to his private apartments.

And this is what she read:

"Beloved of my heart — there now remains only one man's life between you and me. When therefore you have done what you have to do, send me word and I will come to you. I write this in the Cyrillic, as none of the fools about you can read it."

The Grand Master covered his face.

"He should be grievously punished in the person of his dead body," he said, "and the whole Order should bear the disgrace."

"But he is gone to his punishment," said the Abbess. "Be wise and leave the rest to God."

"Yes. We will burn the letter, and leave the rest to God."

"Only young Brother Richard's innocence must be proclaimed for all to know."

"Assuredly."

"And you will restore him to his place in the Order?"

"Most certainly. For it seems to me that he must be a young man of great faith."

IV.
IN
A
GLASS
DARKLY ⸺⸺⸺⸺⸺⸺⸺⸺⸺⸺⸺⸺

The Abbess of Shaston roused herself from her siesta. She was almost certain she had heard someone crying outside her door. But when she opened her door, there was no one there.

The heat of the sun was beginning to abate a little over Jerusalem, and the bells of the Convent of the Holy Alabastron sounded for Nones. Not the Abbess's own convent — she was only a visitor there, by courtesy of the Reverend Mother, the Princess Jovetta, the reigning Abbess. Among the hundreds of convents and monasteries in Jerusalem at the time of the Crusades, the Convent of the Holy Alabastron at Bethany was an important one, although small. It claimed to possess the shards of Mary Magdalene's alabaster box of ointment; and it had been founded some eighteen years before by Queen Melisende herself, for her sister, the Princess Jovetta, whom, though young, she had appointed Abbess. Very royal were these sisters — four in all, the daughters of Baldwin II, King of Jerusalem. One, Hodierna, was Countess of Tripoli; another, Alice, was the wife of the Prince of Antioch, and a better man than that Prince; and Melisende was now Queen of Jerusalem in her own right, with her husband a puppet King. The Abbess Jovetta had a right to consider herself important. Yet the Abbess Hodierna of Shaston was more powerful in her own way, and less was known about her.

She travelled back and forth between England and Palestine just as she pleased, and sometimes disappeared for long periods together. England might think she was in the Holy Land, and the Holy Land might think she was in England — or France, or Italy, or the land of Prester John for that matter. She was fabulously rich, and related to all the influential people in Europe and Outremer, including the Pope. And she knew — what didn't she know? And if she chose to conduct both her convent at Shaston and her own life differently from other people, who dared to gainsay her?

Now behind the shadowy shutters of her well-appointed cell, where it was assumed she meditated in the heat of the day, she bathed in cool water, and dressed herself in a shift of thin linen, and over it a habit, of conventional cut indeed, but of the thin but dense white silk the Saracen women wrapped themselves in; it veiled her discreetly from head to foot, and a blue-lined veil set off the gleaming white gorget and wimple that framed her face, and yet it billowed comfortably round her in the heat. Not for her the wool and serge and frieze, not to mention the hair-shirts, of the Sisters of the Alabastron. She frequently said that she did not see how God was glorified by prickly heat, impetigo, and the itch.

So she went down, just in dignified time, to the chapel, where the office of Nones was sung.

When she returned, she heard the same sound of crying just as she reached her door, and turned quickly. There was a young nun, a novice, crouching in the corner by the door, with the edge of her black veil over her face. The girl clutched at the Abbess's robe.

"Oh, let me speak to you, Reverend Mother — but alone . . ."

The Abbess drew her inside her own chamber, and shut the door.

"Now, my child. Oh, don't look so frightened. Let me see you. What's your name, then?"

"Sister Melisende, Reverend Mother."

"Oh, yes. Drop that veil. Take it right off. Yes, on your obedience. And let me have a good look at you."

It was a sweet face, with the magnolia skin, the rounded outlines, the deeply marked brows, that showed Armenian blood, yet not altogether Armenian. The Abbess considered her thoughtfully.

"Oh, yes, child, I can guess what it is. Am I right?"

A deep sob was the answer.

"Now, now. No need to panic. Who is he?"

"Brian Fitz-Fulke, knight of the Lord Joscelin of Tripoli."

"I know him. Oh, a decent enough young man. Well, what do you want me to do?"

"Oh, Reverend Mother," the girl cried, falling on her knees — "only this. If I must be immured, let them strangle me first!"

The Abbess laid her hand on the girl's bowed head. "Nonsense, child. They won't do anything of the kind to you. That's never done now, no matter what the stories say. Don't be frightened. Now, how many months is it?"

"Four, Reverend Mother."

"And do you want to keep the child, or . . . ?"

"Oh, I want to keep it but how could I?"

"So much the better. I respect you the more." The girl looked up sharply, surprised. "Would the young fellow marry you, do you think?"

"Oh, yes, yes, I'm sure he would. He has said so. But how could we?"

"How? We'll have to see. Now what about your parents?"

"Reverend Mother, I have no parents. I was a foundling, left on the doorstep of this convent, so they tell me. No one cares for me except — except our own Abbess, and, oh, Reverend Mother, it's she I fear most of all! She says I belong to her body and soul — under God, of course. She loves me, I know, but so fiercely. When she knows, I think she'll kill me with her own hand."

"Indeed? And you, child, did you ever want to be a nun? I can see you don't now, but had you ever a vocation?"

"Why, I'd no choice. What else could I possibly be?"

"I see. Well, now, my child, stop worrying and run along to your duties. Trust me to do what I can for you. Say nothing to anyone, but leave it all to me. No, don't grovel at my feet. Bless you, poor thing. Run along."

When she had gone, the Abbess cogitated deeply. Faces and looks — and ages and dates. Presently she rang her little silver bell, and when an obsequious lay-sister came, she bade her take word to the Lady Abbess of the convent that the Lady Abbess of Shaston would like her to come and take a cup of wine with her that evening after Compline.

The two Abbesses greeted each other with elaborate ceremony, each sinking to the ground with a sweeping of skirts.

"My dear Reverend Mother Jovetta."

"My dear Reverend Mother Hodierna."

Jovetta, the Abbess of the Alabastron, Princess of Jerusalem, was older, it would seem, than the Abbess of Shaston. The Abbess Jovetta could not have been more than forty, yet she looked sixty. Men and women aged quickly in Outremer if they survived into middle age at all. Jovetta had the look of one designed to be opulent, even fleshy, but fallen away to a near skeleton; her skin, once magnolia-creamy, lay shrunken into folds and ridges; her great dark eyes looked out from blue hollows, deep and wide-spaced, under her broad brows. She must have been very beautiful once. Now her eyebrows were grizzled and straggling, and there was a little hair on her upper lip. Her mouth was tense, and her movements stiff and constrained. The thick wool habit weighed her down.

Both Abbesses were attended by a retinue of two nuns of their own Orders, but they dismissed them, and the Abbess of Shaston drew the other to a comfortable chair.

"A cup of Cyprus wine? As I am your guest, I feel you should be my guest sometimes, dear sister. Sweet or dry? Oh, but you should drink more wine, you know. Moderation in all things, even in abstinence."

Jovetta replied formally, uneasily sipping the Cyprus wine as they sat by the lattice overlooking the enclosed garden below. She was wondering why the Abbess Hodierna had sent for her. Not just to drink Cyprus wine.

"I have sent for you," she said, "to show you something. A new toy. Something a merchant brought me from beyond Persia."

Jovetta's bushy eyebrows went up a little.

"Your toys are wont to be devilish, my dear Hodierna."

"Oh, not at all, not at all. This will stand any amount of holy water. I can't think why people have these strange ideas about me. Devilish? Why, no. Do you really think so?" She turned a face of sunshine on the frowning Jovetta.

"Why, after all, if the truth were known," she went on, getting no reply, "I've met the Devil, and dealt with him. His dark lordship had the worst of the encounter, I think!" She laughed.

"You mean, of course," said Jovetta, "that you met and overcame Temptation?"

"M — m — m, in a way. Perhaps not quite like that. Oh, some day perhaps, I'll tell you the story for the good of your soul. Very attractive, he was." She smiled, shaking her head. The other crossed herself.

"But for these small sleights," Hodierna went on, "there's no power of devils in them. Nothing but study and attention. A skill, like any other. So let me show you."

She closed the solid shutters over the lattice, and drew a curtain over them. The room was now lit only by a hanging lamp of many-coloured glass. Now she took from a cabinet a strange object — a mirror, yet not a mirror. It was about two feet across, perfectly round, and made of polished black stone, smooth, but not reflecting, a deep pool of blackness. It hung between two uprights like pillars. Hodierna set it carefully upon a table, and placed their two chairs where both could sit and look at it comfortably. She moved in the half-dark quietly and smoothly, saying nothing, and the room seemed to grow very silent as she took her place and composedly sat down.

"Now look at the black mirror, look steadily, and you will see pictures. No need to tell me what you see, for I shall see it too."

The Abbess Jovetta looked, but before she saw anything she heard a child crying. A little girl, she saw her now, was weeping bitterly. Her three big sisters stood round her trying to console her. They were so big and she so little.

"But why do I have to go?" the little girl was saying. She seemed to be cloaked and ready for a journey. Outside the stone arch of the doorway horses and litters were waiting. "Why have I got to go to Father in Kharpurt? What does he want me for? He never wants me other times."

"Ah, you see," the eldest sister was saying, "Father's the King, never forget it. The Saracens have taken him in battle, and imprisoned him in Kharpurt, and of course we must get him back. So he's promised the Saracens a part of the lands and city of Antioch, and a great deal of money, and you have to go and live among the Saracens for surety until the lands are handed over and the money paid, so that he can come home."

"A hostage," said one of the other sisters incautiously, but the eldest turned hastily and hushed her.

"Count Joscelin's nephew goes with you," the eldest sister went on. "He's to remain there too. You mustn't let him see you cry. Be sure we shall be expecting your return. We'll watch your rights and your interests. If anyone wrongs you, let *me* know. We daughters of Baldwin stand together."

A large dark-faced nurse came and swept her mantle round the little girl, obliterating the picture. Presently the folds of the cloak became the curtains of a travelling litter. Those who watched seemed to feel the swaying and bumping. The little girl was desperately tired. The curtains parted and a boy's face looked in, making a horrible, frightening grimace. The little girl shrieked, and the boy laughed and disappeared. The next thing was a dead rat on a stick, thrust in through the curtains — then a toad, its leathery legs dangling down. "Oh, don't you like it?" came the mocking voice. "Next time I'll bring a snake." He was a horrible boy, always doing things to frighten her. "Oh, but it's all right," she could hear him explaining to the guards round the litter. "I'm only amusing the Princess — just cheering her up. Like it? Of course she likes it." It was a hateful journey. The poor little Princess had no mother to yearn for, but often she longed for her three big sisters, in their white stone house by the sea.

Then she was going in at the gateway of a great stony castle, up ever so high; the doorway was cut in a peculiar curve, and across it ran an inscription in the Saracen language. A big bearded Saracen was handing her from her litter. Her father stood close beside him, and with him was a boy a little older than herself.

The Abbess Hodierna heard the quick intake of breath, and from the corner of her eye saw the Abbess Jovetta's hands tighten on her lap.

The little girl was being led forward. Her father embraced her tenderly. This was unusual, the little girl reflected. Her father had never been particularly affectionate to any of them, to her least of all. But here he was acting as if she were the darling of his heart. He was blond and red-faced, with his yellowish moustache and his plaits of tow-coloured hair falling from under his round steel casque: Baldwin II, King of Jerusalem, now a king in captivity.

"My lord Timurtash," he was saying, "here is my most beloved youngest daughter, the Princess Jovetta. She is the very apple of my eye, the adored companion of my age." (Liar, thought the little Jovetta.) "I, being King of Jerusalem, must needs go back to my kingdom, which requires me urgently. You, my Lord Timurtash, are so courteous as to let me purchase my freedom, for the portion of Antioch beyond Orontes, and the sum of money named. Now, in pledge of the payment thereof, I leave here my beloved daughter with you, until the money shall have been paid and the city and lands handed over. With her I leave the young Fulke, the son of my brother-in-arms, Joscelin Count of Tripoli. So, my darling —" (and he turned and bowed before the little Jovetta) "you will remain here, but not for long. You can be sure that the money, the lands, and the city will soon be handed over, and you will return to me, my beloved daughter, to gladden my heart in Jerusalem."

Everyone applauded, and some of the old men wiped away tears with their robes, and King Baldwin and Timurtash clasped hands. And the frightened little Jovetta was led away. And now Jovetta the Abbess, watching tensely, upright in her chair, could have no doubt but that this Jovetta was herself. Dimly the pictures rose in her mind, and the mirror before her lit up the faint images, coloured them in, presented them to all her senses.

She saw how long she had waited for her father to come and fetch her home. She saw how Fulke used to torment her, saying that their release would never come. How they would keep her there forever and marry her to a Saracen and make a Moslem of her, and then her soul would be damned and she would go to hell. As she grew older, too, he was always trying to tell her about other things, things she didn't want to know. Till one day, as she was running away from him, in tears, through the flower gardens, Timurtash's nephew, the young Nur-ed-Din, had stopped her pursuer and fought him and driven him off, and then come back and comforted her.

Then she saw, clearly pinpointed in the mirror, a day when messengers arrived at the court of Timurtash. He had sent them to King Baldwin demanding the payment of his promise.

"This is the answer of my Lord Baldwin," the messenger declaimed. "I have no money to pay the ransom you demanded of me. Antioch is not in my power to bestow, and the Prince of Antioch commands me to hold the city against you. I have fortified it and will hold it. Defiance to you therefore. Given by me, Baldwin the Second, King of Jerusalem."

An angry murmur went round the assembly. Timurtash, seated cross-legged on his divan, frowned above his black beard.

"So — the hostages are forfeit. Let none lay hands on the Princess Jovetta. She stays here with me, and I will be a kinder father to her than was her own. But Fulke of Tripoli shall pay for all."

She saw Fulke turn white, and stretch out imploring hands, but only to have manacles put on them. "Slow or sudden?" a man asked Timurtash. "Sudden and merciful," he replied. Fulke was let out and the whole assembly sighed. And the young Princess burst into tears, though she had never loved Fulke.

The scene became a garden, the green enclosed garden in the heart of Timurtash's fortress. Palms and flowering bushes made a deep shade, all enclosed by the columns and arches overlaid with glittering mosaics, where the long trailing verses of the Koran flourished everywhere. The green shadows filled the space as if it had been a cistern of cool water, and in the midst was a tiny fountain, and pale lilies blooming in the coolness. And here, as Jovetta sat weeping, Nur-ed-Din came to her.

The picture in the mirror seemed to spread out and enclose the watcher, till she was inside the picture, and was the picture. A strain of music, it seemed — or was it perfume? — came to her, and wrenched at her heart. The green garden was blotted out, overwhelmed, with roses — drifting rose-petals, sweet beyond words, covering the picture as they covered her eyes. Soft voices came through.

"Jovetta, beloved — "

"Nur-ed-Din — Nureddin — doesn't it mean the Light of Faith?"

"The light of *The* Faith, beloved. And my faith is different from yours. Yet I will keep faith with you. Even unto death."

"Don't speak of death. But what shall we do, love, what shall we do?"

"We will go away by night, secretly, to a place in the mountains. A place I know. There you will live in peace, and there our child will be born."

"But let it be soon, beloved."

"Oh, yes, it shall be soon."

And then the rose-petals melted away, and she was standing before Timurtash. He was smiling, but sadly.

"So I must say good-bye to you, my dear daughter from among the strangers. I am sending you home to the Franks. Are you not glad to go? Of course you are. Your father is dead. Oh, no tears for that hypocrite, child. You know he never loved you. And your sister Melisende is now Queen of Jerusalem, and her husband holds the crown by her right. I would have peace now between us and the Kingdom of Jerusalem, so I am sending you back. Surely you are glad to go? And to make the embassage more honourable, I send my nephew Nur-ed-Din to escort you to your home. Go, and may Allah go with you."

A journey in sorrow and fear. A dozen times, as he bent over her litter, she whispered to him, "Couldn't we break away here, and fly through the desert to the mountains?" But Timurtash's men guarded them too closely.

She saw herself entering the great portal of the royal palace in Jerusalem. A lingering glance was the only farewell she could take of Nur-ed-Din. She was sitting, forlorn and tired, on a cushioned chair in the women's chamber, and got unsteadily to her feet as her sister entered — the formidable Melisende, the big sister, now Queen of Jerusalem. As she stood up, her loose garments billowed around the curves of her body. Melisende caught her in her arms, and ran her hands quickly over her.

"Oh, my sister — oh, my beloved sister — oh, but Jovetta, how is it with you? My poor, poor child. Did the Saracens rape you, then?"

Frightened and overwhelmed, Jovetta could only nod her head mutely.

"Shame on them! Shame, shame and vengeance! Bloody vengeance! That they should treat a daughter of Baldwin so, and send her back thus. Guards, there!"

Two armed men appeared at the door.

"The escort and embassage from the Saracens are still within the castle. Let them be killed, every one!"

Jovetta found her voice at last. She fell on her knees, clinging to Melisende.

"Oh, no, no! At least not Nur-ed-Din. It was not rape. Nur-ed-Din loved me."

"*Loved* you? He dared? Oh, worse shame. Guards, let it be as I said. Every one of them! So we avenge the affront to a daughter of Baldwin. And so much for their embassage of peace!"

Outside there were shouts, and the grinding of swords.

The Abbess Jovetta sprang to her feet, shaking, holding the arm of her chair.

"I'll see no more of this. I can't bear it . . ."

"Sit down," came the other Abbess's voice, very low and steady. "There is one more picture you *must* see."

And the one more picture was of Jovetta, in tears, leaning over a cradle.

As the Abbess Jovetta sank in her chair, her veil drooping over her face, the Abbess Hodierna took the mirror from its stand, laid it aside, and lit two wax candles. In their light, the Abbess Jovetta showed a ravaged face.

"Why have you shown me this . . . this fable? I will never forgive you."

"*I* did not show it, my dear Reverend Mother. The mirror itself showed it. And as for why, there's a poor little wench of a novice whose name is Melisende — yes, her godmother's name — who tells me you are wont to say she belongs to you body and soul. A poor little thing who only knows that she was left on the doorstep of this convent — as indeed she was, but not in the way that she supposes. No one, dear Reverend Mother, belongs to anyone body and soul; each one belongs to God. But you, I think, are responsible for her body — and perhaps for her soul also."

Jovetta sat pale and tremulous.

"What do you want me to do?"

"Why, I think it would be advisable, only advisable, to absolve the poor girl from her vows. After all, she had no choice, had she? And she'll never make a nun. You might very well set her free, and arrange for her to marry young Brian Fitz-Fulke, of the household of the Count of Tripoli — a name I think you remember? And also I think it would be fitting if you gave her a generous dowry. She *said* she belonged to you body and soul."

Jovetta gave a great sigh. "It shall be done. God knows I've loved that girl. But I had forgotten, or

— 90 —

perhaps did not want to remember." She suddenly looked up. "But how do I know all this is true? The spirit of the mirror could tell lies."

"Oh, no, I think not, dear Jovetta. The mirror shows you what is in your own mind. And not only that. You forget, perhaps, my name is Hodierna, the name of your other sister. She was my godmother. We god-sibs have but few secrets from each other."

V.
WITH
A
LONG
SPOON _____

The Abbess of Shaston was bored. So she decided to raise the Devil.

It was unusual for her to be bored — she had so many interests, and such ample means of pursuing them. What with her extensive lands, and her deep studies, and her strange and much-rumoured disguises, her travels to and from Outremer, and her political manipulations . . . nor was that all . . . and of course, the proper conduct of the religious life in her convent of Shaftesbury in her beloved Wessex.

But at the immediate moment she was not able to do very much, being a guest in the house of her fellow-Abbess, the royal lady Jovetta, Abbess of the Holy Alabastron in Bethany. The Abbess Jovetta followed her rule very strictly, and there were so many things one couldn't do. There one had to sit, in the hot weather, just outside the Holy City of Jerusalem, it being the middle time of the Crusades — most of the knights away on campaigns, and the surrounding country not really safe to venture into without the help of disguises for which she hadn't the means handy — oh, and all sorts of reasons why things couldn't be done.

So the Abbess decided to have a try at raising the Devil.

She had various books with her, Grimoires and the like, and carefully read up her technique beforehand. She took great care to select from among the numerous methods. She rejected anything really dangerous — that is, anything requiring her to abjure her faith, or affront the Powers Above, or commit herself to any allegiance to the Powers Below. She didn't intend to go all the way. Just a little experiment. Eventually she found a method, sure and reliable, that seemed suitable; and having procured what was necessary, she made her preparations.

She gave out that she intended to make a three days' retreat for prayer and devotion, in the guest quarters to which the Abbess Jovetta had assigned her. Though it was known as her "cell," it was a very comfortable suite of rooms giving on a pleasant enclosed garden, walled all round, opening with a small wicket gate on the wild country beyond, and not overlooked. She had a spacious parlour with a marble floor, and here she cleared all furniture back to the walls, and in the clear space set up her circle, with her brazier, herbs, holy water, dagger and cup, and all the rest of it, within the circle; and proceeded according to the book. It was about sunset on a Saturday when she began her conjurations — a warm, still summer evening. But after a full two hours by the convent bells, nothing had happened.

"Oh, well," she said to herself, "it seems it just doesn't work. No matter," and she broke her circle, put all the apparatus carefully away, and stepped out into the garden.

The garden was very beautiful in the moonlight. The high walls sheltered it from all but the lightest breezes; tall palms drooped overhead, their fronds hardly moving, and below them, in the blue-green dimness, white flowers bloomed — lilies and fantastic bell-shaped moonflowers that gave off an intoxicating scent. Beside them was the mystery of a deep-red rose, black in the strange light, yet somehow keeping the secret of its crimson. She moved slowly across the garden, and then — someone knocked at the wicket gate.

"Who is it?" she asked sharply. A man's voice replied, "May I come in? You called me."

Her heart beat violently.

"Oh, yes, come into the garden," she said, and opened the wicket gate.

The man who entered was tall and richly dressed. He moved with a royal grace, swinging a long dark cloak behind him. His face was powerful, formidable, yet strangely handsome in a swarthy and shadowed way, with intensely black hair and a little neat black beard. His dress was the usual court dress of a knight, but he wore no distinguishing blazon. Jewels glinted at his ears and on his long well-shaped fingers. He bowed low over her hand, as the wicket gate clicked shut behind him.

"Madame."

"Sir. What may I call you?"

"My name for the present," said he, "is the Sieur Janicot de Partout."

"Then, Sieur Janicot de Partout, I bid you welcome."

"And what, dear lady, do you ask of me?"

"Why . . . nothing," she said.

"Nothing?" He frowned a little. "But Madame, is it possible you have wasted my time?"

"Oh, sir!" she laughed reproachfully. "That is not a very gallant thing to say to a lady who has invited you into her garden!"

"Oh, your pardon, Madame. Believe me, I do appreciate your invitation. But it is usual for such an invitation to have a purpose . . . ?"

She looked at him with a very sweet smile.

"I just wanted to meet you. To see what you were like. Mere female curiosity. But I'd hate to think I'd wasted your time."

"So?" He smiled back at her. "And since I am here, what do you think of me? What am I like, then?"

"A gentleman," she said.

He gave a little bow. "Then will you not invite me into your pleasant little parlour yonder?"

"Oh, pardon me, but I think not," she said, remembering that she had broken up and released the Circle. "You might find things there that were not to your liking." (After all, it would be bad manners to confront him with a crucifix!) "And on the other hand, I must not bring you under the same roof with my girls, now must I? They are far too young. Or rather, not *my* girls, but my sister Jovetta's girls. Or come to that, my sister Jovetta. Though possibly she has encountered you already."

"Possibly," he said, smiling and showing his white teeth. "But only, of course, in a metaphysical sense."

"Come," said she, turning away from the door leading into the convent building, "let us walk in the garden. It is very pleasant there."

"Yes, let us walk in the garden," he assented, and offered her his right arm. She laid her hand lightly upon it, and he placed his left hand, softly and warmly, on hers.

The sensation was wonderful. A deep sensuous warmth spread from his hand, sending a thrill all over her body. Careful, she said to herself. I must be careful. But it's delicious – forbidden fruit – oh yes, I can look at it, smell it, perhaps caress its velvet surface, but never taste it. Meantime, enjoy, enjoy. But careful, careful.

They strolled together in the moonlight, along the smooth-tiled paths, between the formal dwarf hedges of lavender, under the palms. For anyone who could have seen them, they made an impressive pair – he in his falling dark cloak, red or black in the bluish light, she in glimmering white falling straight from head to foot.

"Permit me to say, Madame," said the dark gentleman, "that I am greatly honoured that you should invite me here. I am not often invited consciously and sincerely." He sighed. "Those that invite me in so many words usually do not want me at all. But such an attractive woman as you are, Madame — !"

He pressed her hand. Oh, delightful, delightful, she thought to herself, thrilling to the roots of her hair. But careful, careful.

"You are very flattering, sir."

"Indeed I do not flatter, Madame. I am greatly attracted to you. But attractive as your body is, there is something else I desire far more. Your beautiful soul. You have a most remarkable, strangely gifted soul. In return for it, I would give you anything you cared to name. Anything!"

Now, she thought to herself. Oh yes, here it comes, his fair offer. Just to sell my soul. My soul is myself, and *he* wants it so that he can change it, pervert it. Whatever quality a man values and admires, that he must lose. The man who values courage must become a coward, the one who admires compassion must become a brute. He who loves loyal friendship must become a betrayer of friends. Oh, I know your methods, my noble lord.

"Come now," he was saying, "you know my powers. What do you wish for?"

Don't ask him for anything, she thought. If you ask for anything he'll give it to you, and the bargain will be made, and you'll be lost. The thrill of his touch began to cool, and she withdrew her hand from his arm.

"Well, now," she said lightly, "first let me know what you have to offer."

"Oh!" he laughed. "How like a lady. You want to look round before you buy. Very well then, let's see. First of all, there's Beauty. Most of you ladies want that."

"Thank you," she said, "but I think I have sufficient good looks already. Don't you think so?"

"*Touché*!" and his smile broadened. "I've already admitted that you are attractive, and I'm considered a judge. How could I say that you lacked anything? Oh, but such immortal beauty as I could give you — and to last forever!"

Against the glimmering dark green of the palms in front of her, a mist seemed to form, and on it a picture, a picture of a face of such surpassing beauty as was never seen on earth. The picture grew and extended, till she could see the whole form: lightly clothed, adorned with the most glorious jewels, which yet did not distract from the wonderful face and body.

The Abbess knew she was looking at herself, transfigured. One moment the picture hung like a shadow on a screen of raindrops, and then it was gone.

She turned her eyes back to the dark gentleman.

"Well?" he said.

"Oh, very beautiful, very lovely. But no, I thank you. I have never heard of a woman yet who was the happier for more than her due share of beauty. I do not wish to be another Helen of Troy."

"As you wish, but to keep the looks you have, for many, many years, perhaps forever, how would that be?"

She appeared to consider. "All very fine, but I should be cut off from my generation, like that poor Wandering Jew. Century after century, unable to pass through the Other Door. And a young face I might have, but how old my heart would grow! No, thank you, sir. I will not have everlasting beauty and youth in this world. I have to consider the Next."

His fine black eyebrows shot up.

"So? Then we must think of something different. Let us walk again. Please take my arm." She took his arm again, and once more felt the strange, exciting current. Playing with fire, she said to herself. Could she keep sufficient command to drop it before it burned her?

"There are other things," he went on. "For one thing, there is Wealth. So many people want that. Would you not like to be as rich as I could make you?"

"Thank you," she said demurely, "but I am already sufficiently rich. You know the saying — if the Abbess of Shaston wedded the Abbot of Glaston, their progeny would own more land than the King of England. I think I have enough and should not covet more."

"You are modest," he said with his charming smile. "Your requirements are simple. But that is not wealth. Look!"

And again the airy picture hung before her like a spider's web.

She saw a palace with wide marble floors, and herself seated upon a throne. People were bringing wonderful things before her. First were gowns — velvets like the downy skin of peaches, silks and lawn so fine that they floated high in the air like vapour. It seemed that she could feel the lovely textures. In a vast oval mirror she saw herself in garments made of all these stuffs in turn, strangely fashioned; and other garments of soft warm wool, even more richly coloured than the silks. She felt a gentle touch at her side, and there was a girl holding a casket, where in a nest of silk, faintly rose-tinted, there lay coiled ropes and ropes of pearls, all perfect, all white as drops of cream. The girl held the casket while she ran her fingers over them, picked them up in hand-fuls, caressed them, displayed them against her bo-som and her arms. But her hands, she saw, were already ablaze with jewels. Not only rounded rubies like drops of blood, and sapphires like the night sky, but other gems she had not seen before — white adamants cut into facets like tiny mirrors, so that each one blazed like the sun . . . all up her arms were bracelets that shimmered with such gems, and round her neck more jewels glittered.

A movement drew her eyes away, and there on a divan were heaped furs, more rich than any she had seen or heard of — skins of strange and beautiful beasts, supple as fine cloth, the delicate hairs bristling softly — leopards and tigers and northern white bears, and the soft grey hair of squirrels. She ran her hands through them all. Then there were people that brought her great baskets of flowers, of new and exciting kinds, of unknown colours and shapes and fragrances; and fruits, from far away, offering their luscious juices. Just in time she remembered not to taste, but that was hard. She had to content herself with smelling their deliciousness. Enchanting little animals were brought for her to play with, furry small beasts like kittens but much, much more beautiful. Clasping one such in her arms, and trailing her silken robes, she stepped slowly down the wide marble steps to where a boat, a beautiful boat, floated easily on a shining lagoon, all ready for the strong rowers to take her anywhere, anywhere in the wide wonderful world, and safely back again. There was more, there was more waiting for her to enjoy, but . . .

Softly it all broke up, and dissolved into raindrops. The dark man was smiling at her. "Well?"

She sighed. "Oh, it was beautiful! I did enjoy it so much. Thank you for letting me see it all. But no, thank you. I will not choose it."

"No?" he said, surprised. "But why not? I can show you more if that isn't enough."

"Why not?" said she. "Oh, just because I feel the price is a little too high."

"Well, then, we must consider something else. All women want Love, do they not?"

She avoided his eye.

"You know I am vowed to religion."

"Yes, I know — and Lady, forgive me, but I know a great deal else besides."

She drew back and flashed out at him in anger.

"Then you will leave all that alone."

He saw his mistake.

"I do crave your pardon. I would not be so ungentlemanly. Forgive me. But let us consider what is past. Dear Lady, the tender memories of the past are not subject to reproach. If I were to turn time back, and restore to you certain times, certain en-counters, certain moments now lost . . . if I were to give back to you some whose names are written in your heart."

Against her will she felt tears spilling down her cheeks. Pictures rose, faces and voices.

"No," she said, tremulous but resolute. "Such things would only be a mockery. I should go mad living amongst phantoms."

"As you wish, Lady. We will not consider Love. But what of Power?"

"Power?" Dry-eyed again she met his look smiling. "I think I have power. All over Europe and Outremer I pull a string here and a string there, and their jealous crusading princes and barons rise and fall at my bidding — when I need them to, and when I can give myself the trouble. Everyone knows that behind them all it is I, the Abbess of Shaston. What more power do I want?"

"Ah, yes, Madame, but look what might be. Power to do all the good in the world that you would like to do."

Again the misty curtain hovered, and the picture became clear. The Abbess saw herself on a high throne, and before her came all the afflicted of the world — the diseased, the lame, the blind, the distressed, the hideous. From her hands flowed Virtue, and she saw them go away healed and happy. Outside her palace they danced for joy on the steps. Away from her, as it were rivers flowing, went messengers at her mandate, to comfort misery all over the world — to pacify warring peoples, to rebuild ruined cities, to bring prosperity to the poor.

Watching it, the Abbess felt her heart expand with the beauty of the perfect peace she might be able to give. She was almost ready to cry, "Yes, yes, my soul is yours for the sake of this, the power to do universal good!" But she watched further. The people who had been healed and helped poured their praises at her feet, and at the feet of the one that stood behind her. She herself bathed in their thanks and flattery. Then she noticed that the stream of miserable ones who came to beseech her grew never less, but still flowed.

"Your lordship," she said, "how is it that the stream of misery never dries up? The sicknesses return, the wars break out again. I do not see one evil being healed at its source and done away with."

"Why," he said with a little laugh, "you would not have us abolish the reason for all our good work? Dear Lady, in some five hundred years from now, a poet will write:

> Pity would be no more
> If there were nobody poor —
> And Mercy could not be
> If all were as happy as we:
> So Misery's increase
> Is Mercy, Pity, Peace.

Lady, we must not altogether cure the evils we heal."

It seemed to her, then, that the power of benevolence that went out from her on the throne where she saw herself had, as it were, a curve. It turned upon itself and went back and back. But all redounded to her glory, and that of the Dark Man behind her.

"No," she said, "no and no and no! In the end it would not be good. My dear sir, I reject your offer, totally and finally."

"So?" He loosed her arm and turned to face her, frowning. "Madame, I have made you a number of very good offers, and none of them seems to please you."

"I know, but I have enjoyed seeing them so much," she said sweetly.

"Then will your ladyship tell me, once and for all, what you really want?"

"Yes," she said, and lifted limpid eyes to him. "The Kingdom of Heaven."

Suddenly there was a violent hissing sound as of water thrown on hot coals, and a flash of red light, in which she saw the stranger's face transformed into a mask of such hideous malignity, that she staggered backwards and nearly fell.

Almost at once the stranger recovered his poise and his appearance.

"Oh, I am sorry, Madame. For a moment I lost my temper. So unlike me. Forgive my unfortunate lapse."

"I think I had better say goodnight to you, sir," she said mastering her tremor, though her voice still shook a little. "It has been a very pleasant evening's entertainment, but it is over, and I think very soon the cocks will begin to crow. I thank you, and wish you a good journey to — wherever it is you go." She did not hold out her hand to him, but she opened the wicket gate. "*Depart in Peace*, and I do not think you should call on me again." He bowed and went out without a word. She carefully shut the wicket gate, and made over it the sign of the cross, and also the Pentagram.

She sighed a little. It had all been so enjoyable.

Then from a clump of lignum-vitae bushes beside the wicket gate, there stepped out a very tall, thin, golden young man in a long white robe.

"You took a very great risk, Madame-my-child," he said.

"Oh," she said laughing, "I knew you were there all the time."

"You did, did you? And do you think of the trouble you give us?" replied her guardian angel.

"Oh, I do beg your pardon," she said, "But you see, I have absolute faith."

He frowned, shaking his smooth blond head.

"Pride, and presumption, and tempting Providence. Absolute faith, my . . . wings!" said the guardian angel.

VI.
A
QUESTION
OF
TASTE _____

The elderly Templar who had been instructed to
escort and guide the Abbess of Shaston whenever
she went riding in the wilderness of Judaea, would
gladly have been fighting the Saracens instead. Not
that the company of the Abbess was unattractive. It
was, on the contrary, very attractive indeed, but the
responsibility of taking care of her was too great. To
say she was a strong-willed lady, and unpredictable,
was an understatement. She herself had made it
quite clear that she did not want an escort, but she
was a guest in the house of the other Abbess, the
Princess Jovetta, sister of the great Melisende, Queen
of Jerusalem in her own right.

The Abbess Jovetta ruled the Convent of the
Holy Alabastron, at Bethany, and was always glad —
or was she? — to give hospitality to Hodierna, Abbess
of the Convent of Saint Evodias and Saint Syntyche,
of Shaftesbury in Wessex, on her frequent pilgrim-
ages to the Holy Land. Now, ever since the time that
Hodierna had disappeared into the wilderness for a
whole week, and came back in the company of the
shaggy Satyrs, Jovetta had insisted on an escort for
her of one Knight Templar, his two squires, and two

nuns. Not exactly conducive to freedom and solitude. And, as been said, no sinecure for poor Sir
Hugh the Knight Templar.

She would always ride too fast and too far. She
was doing so now, and heading straight for the
dangerous country, on the slopes of the Lebanon,
where the Old Man of the Mountains, the lord of the
Assassins, had his secret fortress.

"Madame, I think we had better turn back," he
said, panting somewhat in the late afternoon sun. He
could hardly keep up with her.

"No, no," she replied over her shoulder, smiling,
and went galloping on. She rode astride, as Queen
Eleanor had done. Queen Eleanor, as everyone
knew, had worn leather breeches like a man, with a
boy's short tunic over them, and had designed simi-
lar dress for the ladies of her retinue, when she had
accompanied King Louis of France, her first husband, on his crusade. The Abbess rode boldly astride
her fine Arab horse, with her cool white robes
flowing free on each side, but Heaven forbid that a
Templar should speculate on what she wore under
those robes. Balanced and straight in the saddle, she
rode at ease, while the poor nuns behind her, riding
decorously side-saddle, were visibly wilting.

With dismay the Templar saw in the distance a
many-coloured group of mounted men approaching
from the mountains.

"Madame," he said urgently, "now you will *have*
to turn back. There's danger — look — Saracens

approaching." She gave a long look under the shade of her hand at the distant horsemen, now coming rapidly nearer.

"Yes. Right! Now you go back all of you, and do not follow me."

Uneasy and puzzled, her small procession halted. She wheeled her horse to face her companions.

"Yes. That is what I said. I am going on. You are to go back and leave me. You are not to follow me."

"But, Lady," the Templar protested, "the danger!"

"*You* will be in very great danger. I shall not. Now, is that clear?"

"What would you do, Lady? Meet the Saracens?"

"Yes. That is what I said. I will rejoin you when my work is done — in a week, or a month. Who knows? Now, once again, is that clear? I don't want any of you to get killed." (Small shrieks from the two nuns.) "Take your hand from your sword, Sir Hugh. *On your obedience* to Holy Church. Is that plain enough? Now go."

And turning her horse again, she rode steadily toward the oncoming Saracens. Her escort, struck into silence, sat on their horses gazing after her. They saw the Saracen riders surround her in a long moving line, circling in toward her, she sitting still in the midst, as they drew closer and closer in.

"I am your prisoner," she said to the Saracens in their own language, speaking it fluently and well. "Now take me to your master, to the honoured

Raschid ed Din Sinan, who is called the Old Man of the Mountains. Look," — she stretched her hands out — "you may bind my hands if you wish. You may also blindfold me if you think it necessary. But you may not touch me otherwise. I am a consecrated woman, and for a man to lay carnal hands on me would be dangerous defilement of him and all of you, and very bad luck as well." She smiled round at the fierce bearded faces.

"Well enough, lady," said one of them who seemed, by his golden collaret and turban jewel, to be in authority. "But we must search you, lest you have a hidden dagger."

"Oh yes, you would think of that. No, I've no weapons, neither have I any money or jewels, or anything of value. But I'll submit to be searched by your women. I presume you have some women in your fortress? And not by eunuchs, either. Meantime you may tie my hands," and she held them out submissively. "But, listen to one word — "

As the captain leant from the saddle to tie her hands, she whispered one word to him. He started back, and looked at her with respect.

"So? Lady, I did not know. I crave your pardon, but I must bind your hands, and — is it permitted to ask where and how you learnt — that Name?"

"It is not permitted," she said, with her finger on her lip. He smiled, and gave an order to the others. They turned all together and rode away toward the mountains, where the pinnacle of the castle of Raschid

ed Din Sinan lost itself among the God-made pin-
nacles of the rocks.

Her frustrated escort stood sadly watching her
and the Saracens till they were out of sight.

It was an amazing thing to find, in the heart of
that stony fortress, a little room like a jewel. It was
perfectly proportioned, leading the eye at once to
the small fountain that occupied the centre, where a
refreshing jet of water sprang up high and fell back
again into a many-coloured marble basin. There
were no windows, but a blaze of light came in from
a cupola above, broken into many colours, and
tempered to a lovely glow as it fell on mosaics of
onyx and jasper, porphyry and coral, nacre and
ebony and chrysoprase, all touched here and there
with gold. Delicately carved niches and arches and
fretted screens surrounded the pool, and a wide
silken divan lay beside its coolness. And here Raschid
ed Din Sinan, the Old Man of the Mountains, rose
from the divan and led the Abbess to a pile of rich
cushions facing him across a low table.

Raschid ed Din Sinan did not, after all, look as
old as she had been led to expect. He might be fifty,
though the stories made out that he had been ruling
there in the mountains for over a hundred years. But
perhaps there had been a succession of men bearing
that name. He had a long black beard, slightly
touched with grey, hanging to his waist. Under the
towering turban of rose-coloured silk with the dia-
mond-spangled plume, his face was lined and watch-

ful, his eyes hooded with heavily wrinkled eyelids. His clothing was gorgeous, more gold than silk, every button a rich piece of the jeweller's art.

He greeted the Abbess with gestures of the greatest respect; she curtsied low and gracefully to him, but was hampered by the delicate golden hand-cuffs — not more than gold bracelets except that they were linked together — that restrained her.

"Oh, but Madame," he exclaimed, "we must not have these," and producing a little gold key he quickly removed them.

"Forgive the zeal of my guards," he said. "Come, I pray you, be seated."

He was charming in manner, she felt, as she settled herself crosslegged on the cushions. Charming but dangerous.

"And what," he asked, "brings the honourable Abbess to give herself so generously into my hands? Does she, perhaps, see the errors of the ways of the Giaours, and wish to exchange the Cross for the Crescent?"

"No, no." She smiled. "Not quite that. Not yet. But I come, honourable Sinan, to sit at your feet and learn of your wisdom."

His face expressed his pleasure. "Lady, you are welcome in the name of Allah the All-Merciful. But tell me, have you been duly prepared to learn the first of the Names?" He smiled as if he had laid a trap for her.

"I know it," she said, and, leaning close to his ear, repeated the word she had said to the captain. He raised his eyebrows, and still more when she added another word.

"Certainly you are prepared for understanding," he said. "But let us take refreshment first." He clapped his hands, and a servant appeared and received instructions, and after a few minutes reappeared with dishes and cups of exquisite porcelain, and a peculiar tall jug with an upward-curving spout. From this the servant poured a hot dark liquid into small cups. The smell of it was delicious.

"None of your people has tasted this before," he said. "But have a care, it is very hot. It is called the Unbeliever's Drink — the 'kafiye.' That is because it warms the heart and excites the blood and the spirits, and therefore the very strict believers are said, by some, to be forbidden it."

She took a cautious sip.

"It is very bitter," she said.

"Ah, then take a mouthful of sweetmeat," — he offered her a dish of loucoum — "and then a sip of iced water — then the kafiye again, then the sweetmeat, then the water, and so on. But do not drink more than half the cupful; the rest is the dregs, and they are muddy . . . now, how is that?"

"Oh, I like it," she said, "but I think it takes some getting used to."

"Do not hurry it. Take time, and inhale its fragrance."

He was watching her, and she knew it. As she set her cup down, suddenly on the floor beside her was a creature — about two spans across, like an octopus but hairy, with a crab's claw at the end of each tentacle. She recoiled, but only for a minute.

"Oh, yes, you're very ugly," she addressed it. "Run away now, you nearly made me drop that pretty cup." She tapped the creature lightly on the head with one finger, as if it were a tiresome child, and traced a pentagram on it. Then she looked back at Sinan, but he was gone. In his place a scaly cobra was sitting coiled against the cushions, reared to strike.

She knew what to do. In an instant she took the shape of a doe — an animal whose long, pointed, horny, cloven hoofs could pin down a snake and batter it to death. Immediately the snake had changed to a great tawny lion, lashing its tail and menacing the doe. In a moment she became the tiniest of grasshoppers, and the lion looked about in disappointment. From the depths of the cushions a human voice came up, breathless but with some laughter.

"Honoured Lord Sinan," it said, "don't let's waste time and energy on this ridiculous game. We both know we can do it, and it's rather fatiguing. Let's call a halt, shall we?"

"Agreed," came the voice from the lion, laughing too. They both resumed their own shapes. The Abbess leaned back against the cushions.

"Oh, it takes a lot of energy in this hot weather," she said. "And besides, it's such an *old* game. Hopelessly out of fashion."

He smiled, showing teeth that were a good deal whiter than the lion's.

"Tell me," she said, "were those illusions — the first one at least — induced by your 'kafiye' drink?"

"No, no," he said. "There are no illusions in the 'kafiye' though it will make the heart beat faster, and keep sleep at arm's length if one needs to keep awake. But the real maker of visions — the opener of the eye of truth — is this, Lady!" From a hidden shelf he took a casket, opened it and held it before her. It was full of small squares of green paste, rather like loucoum, but opaque.

"Is that the famous hashish?" she said.

"It is, Lady. This is the true magic. With this I reward my servants. Will you not try it, Lady?"

"I thank you, no. We in the West abhor such things as you abhor wine."

"Ah, there, Lady, you make a great mistake. You have not tasted our hashish."

"And you have not tasted our wine," she retorted.

"Oh, but I have, and it is sour and unpalatable, and dries up the tongue. And as for your ale, it is loathsome — loathsome. Lady, I would not name to you what it is like."

"Pardon me, honoured sir, but — nonsense!" she laughed. "I can understand your not liking ale — but wine! There are many different kinds. Perhaps what you tasted was an inferior kind?"

He answered rather sulkily, "They said it was the best wine they had . . . certain soldiers whom we captured."

"Oh," she exclaimed, still laughing, "that couldn't have been much good! Look here," she leaned toward him, wagging her forefinger. "There are as many kinds of wine as there are fish in the sea. Now, I could tell you about wines that are sweeter than honey, but not cloying — or sharp as lemons, to refresh one in the heat — or fiery, the very taste of valour — or blent like harmonious chords on the lute. Oh, I could make a drink for you, a cunning mixture, that would ravish your senses like the very fruits of Paradise. A wine that is to all other wines as the rose of Damascus is to all other flowers. I could, indeed I could . . ."

"Could you now?" His mouth seemed to be watering.

"I certainly could. Oh, you would swear you had never tasted any pleasure like it."

"And — would you?"

"A bargain!" she cried. "Come now, I will try your hashish, if you, first, will drink my wonderful wine!"

She could see him swallowing, licking his lips. She could also see him calculating. This lady, so influential, suppose she were a convert to hashish, and in his power, like all those others?

"I agree to your bargain," he said. "But how do you obtain this wonderful wine?"

"I will make it for you. No one else can do that. It will take time, of course — a week, or two weeks, or perhaps three."

He nodded. "But of course, Lady. There would be no question of your leaving us yet."

"And I must have the run of your kitchen."

"I have many kitchens, and you shall have the freedom of them all."

"And many costly ingredients. First, I shall want good cane sugar, also the best Greek honey. Then white grapes, and black grapes, and sweet almonds, and cloves — then apricots, and plums of Persia, and bergamot oranges. Sweet citrons too, and fine fresh eggs — ginger, and eringo root-rosewater, and orange-flower-water — oh, and other things . . ."

Without a doubt his mouth was watering.

"Agreed, Lady, you shall have all you want. And when it is made, I will drink this marvellous drink, and you will partake of our sacred hashish."

"So we shall do," she assured him, and they clasped hands on the bargain.

So she found herself installed in an elegant apartment in the secret palace of the Old Man of the Mountains, with three little girl slaves and a mute eunuch to wait on her, and all the kitchens at her disposal. And all the while she had kept to herself the real business that had brought her there. She had come, not out of curiosity or mischief, but because some days before, a tearful and terrified girl had come to her and implored her to rescue her lover.

Lady Alicia de Hamo, fair-haired and blue-eyed, seventeen — a sweet helpless little thing — and young Conrad Fitzurse, had been recently betrothed, and now he had been captured by the Old Man of the Mountains, who was demanding an inordinate sum for his ransom. His parents had no money. Conrad Fitzurse was a younger son, who had gone out to the Crusades hoping to make his fortune. Lady Alicia's father had fallen at Hattin, and her mother had died not long after, from one of the diabolical fevers that were always with the army, leaving poor Alicia alone in the Holy Land with no protector and no money even to return to England. The Convent of the Alabastron had taken her in, but she would not take the veil, neither had she the required dowry. Then she had met young Fitzurse, and they would have been happily though pennilessly married, Fitzurse hoping that he might yet make his way and his fortune as a knight in arms. And then this blow had fallen on them. According to messages, the Old Man of the Mountains insisted on a large ransom for young Fitzurse, for although the boy had no money, nor had his father, he had an elder brother who had made money enough and to spare. Could not John Fitzurse pay out a few thousand marks for his brother? But John Fitzurse had replied that his brother's troubles were his own fault, and had gone back to

England. Now Alicia lived in daily dread that the ears and fingers would start arriving.

"You can do something," she besought the Abbess. "I know you can. You're so clever, you can do anything."

"My dear," she had replied gently enough, "I can't perform miracles. I'm not a saint."

"A saint? Oh, but you are," the hysterical girl declared.

"No, dear," she said very gravely. "I am certainly not a saint, and it would be very wrong for you to call me so. Indeed, plenty of people would call me something very different."

"Oh, but it's no matter. Whatever they say, I believe in you, dear Reverend Mother. Only do say you'll help me."

"Poor child, I'll do what I can, but God alone knows whether it will be any good."

And with that, Alicia had to be content.

So here the Abbess was at least under the same roof as young Fitzurse. From the kitchens of any castle one learns a great deal of what goes on in the other parts — in the great hall, and the banqueting hall, the harem, the garrison and guardrooms — and in the prisons. She learnt that Conrad was alive and reasonably well. A physician had visited him and treated the wounds he had received during his capture. He was well fed. She contrived to see the food that was sent down to him, but did not dare, as yet, to send any message.

The kitchens were a little world in themselves: a whole long line of them, carved out of the rock below the castle. Two of them were vast caverns, always glowing fiery red ("like the Mouth of Hell," the Abbess thought with awe), where whole sheep and oxen could be roasted on spits the size of jousting lances. Then there were smaller kitchens, with windows that opened on the sheer drop below – a kitchen for fish, another for sweet confections, a dairy and larder very cool and stony, a spicery full of strange exotic smells; a private kitchen for the Old Man's food, another for his Wazir, another for his wives, yet another for his sons, and so on. There were of course innumerable cooks, almost all of whom were disabled in some way. Many were eunuchs, and some were obviously wounded warriors; there were mutes as well, and deaf-mutes, and one blind man who sat all day sieving, pounding and stirring; he would feel textures, and taste pinches of food, with great delicacy. But among them, the Abbess found some who could talk, and would. She learnt that young Conrad was kept in a cell not too far from the kitchen, for more convenience in feeding him. She longed to send him a word of encouragement, but dared not run the least risk of discovery. No smuggling in of tools or weapons, or even of notes. Something might go wrong.

But she got to work with a will, preparing the wonder-drink for the Old Man. She obtained most of the ingredients she asked for, and constantly thought of others that must be obtained. She had enough crucibles, alembics, and stills to set up an alchemist. The work went on, but slowly. One can't hurry a delicate operation of that kind. She had been allotted a tiny kitchen, or pantry, of her own, close to the spicery, and she took care to make friends with the confectioner who worked there.

Her own quarters consisted of a pleasant little stone-flagged chamber, opening on an enclosed garden. Here her meals were served by her little maids. Then, very often the Old Man himself visited her in her garden, and anxiously enquired how the preparation of the drink was going on.

"Slowly, Your Excellency," she said, "slowly but surely. But I need just a little isinglass to clear the mixture," or "just a fragment of ambergris," or "just a few strawberries," and so on.

In the middle of the morning's work she sometimes asked the confectioner to make her the strange "kafiye" drink.

"Look," he said to her, "today I have to make something very special — the pistachio paste for the sacred hashish." He showed her how he ground the green nuts, and mixed them with fine powdered sugar, and bound them with white of egg, mixing in rosewater and various spices — and then how the mixture was pressed into a box, and cooled, and cut into neat cubes, and powdered with yet finer sugar.

"Now this," he said, "has no hashish in it at all. You could eat a boxful — yes, go on, help yourself — and you'll take no harm, unless you surfeit of the sugar. But our master himself keeps the juice of the hashish in his own apartment. With a hollow needle he inserts a drop of it into each square. That is why they must all be of one size. And then — ah, then! — these little green squares become the keys of Paradise to the favoured few to whom he gives them." He lowered his voice. "But some say they are also the keys of hell. Whichever way it is, those who eat of it never get rid of the longing, and become his bondslaves for the rest of their lives. I wouldn't take it if he gave it to me. Though I'm his slave, I prefer to keep my mind free, and not go mad."

"That's very interesting," said the Abbess. "Yes, it's a very nice sweetmeat as it is. May I take another piece?"

"Why, yes — go on, take two. There's plenty here."

And at last the day came when she told the Old Man that her marvellous drink had come to perfection and was ready.

"Tomorrow after midday," he said, "come to my apartment — the room of the fountain — and bring your wonderful drink with you. Then you will eat hashish and I will drink wine, and we shall see what happens."

The gleam in his eye was not such as one ought to direct toward an Abbess. She began to wonder if his interest was entirely confined to the pleasures of the palate.

Carefully she decanted the precious liquid into a very beautiful bottle of gilded glass. It smelt heavenly, like a field of clover in warm sunshine. She tasted the last few drops — yes, it was superb, and powerful. She would dearly have liked to drink an elegant glass of it, but no! above all things she had to keep a clear head. So, with a sigh of regret, she closed it up with its decorative stopper, and carried it carefully to the Old Man's beautiful room.

He was dressed even more gorgeously than usual. "This is a day of festival," he said, bowing low over her hand. "Now, you will take my magic sweetmeat." And he opened the casket of precious paste, and held it out to her. She helped herself to one of the green cubes, and held it in her hand. "And now I will taste your magic drink."

She took a crystal goblet from the table, and poured out her liqueur. His nostrils dilated.

"It smells divine," he said, as he took it from her.

Someone, far back in the Abbess's past, had taught her a juggler's simple trick, the substitution of one thing for another. With her flowing garments it was easy.

They settled themselves amicably side by side on the cushioned divan. He sipped the liqueur.

"By the Prophet, it's marvellous!" he said. "I should rather say, may the Prophet avert his gaze. Oh, but it is delicious . . ."

The Abbess nibbled daintily at the green sweet in her hand. "You must tell me," he said, "when it begins to take effect. Sometimes it is quick, sometimes slow. Tell me of the visions as they arise, until you are able to tell me no more."

She fixed her eyes on the rising and falling jet of water, in the glittering basin before them.

"Oh, my head begins to swim a little — things grow larger — and smaller . . . Honoured Sir, if you find my drink palatable — keep the vessel close by you. Pour out for yourself as you wish, I — my hand may not be steady."

"I will do so," he said, moving the table nearer him, and filling up the glass he had already emptied.

"Oh, by all the creatures of Allah, this is magnificent!" He sipped it delicately — and then less delicately.

She said, "Honoured Sir, are there not goldfish in your fountain? I did not see them before. Why, one of them rises right up the jet — plunges into the air — down again — these are wonderful goldfish, Honoured Sir — large, large, with tails like the wings of birds — they fly out of the water — all round us . . ."

"Marvellous," he said, pouring another glass. "The golden fish-birds of Paradise begin to open the way to you. Soon I shall see them too, Golden birds swimming — fish flying — frying? Flying-fish, great golden ones."

She kept it up.

"Oh, the dome above us. It's gone! There's the blue skies, and the golden clouds of heaven — now I'm flying — the sun — I'm flying right into the sun — oh, I'm afraid of that great furnace — my lord, my lord, what am I to do? Am I to cast myself into the sun?"

"No, my beloved dis—disciple. I know you would if I comman—manded you. 'Senough. Fly downwards now."

"I hear and obey," she said, closing her eyes. "Now I fall down — down, down into such darkness, such darkness — blue, dark, dark blue — there's the sea, and the waves as they break are touched with light. Oh, the waves are over me — lovely waves — they will bear me up, like great whales . . ."

"Leave the waves," he said thickly. "Do as I command you now. Fly back — into — sun — again . . ."

He was lolling back, almost supine on his cushions. She opened her eyes, and glanced quickly at him.

"I am back in the sun, my lord," she said, fixing her eyes on him with a rigid stare. "But the sun does not burn me. I am greater than the sun."

"Goo' girl." His eyes were closed, and his head lolled back and forth on the cushions. "Now come back out of there, and give me more drink." He flapped a hand helplessly toward his empty glass. She rose and filled it for him again, and held it to his lips, raising his head.

"Aah! So do the houris of Paradise raise the heads of the faithful, and re-refresh'em with the delicious . . . delicious . . ." He flung an arm round her and drew her down on the cushions beside him. "Perhaps we are . . . already . . . in Para . . . Para . . ."

"So we are, my lord," she said in her most melodious and soothing voice. "But let me go now," and she rolled him over, and ever so gently disentangled herself. His head fell back again. The rest of the glassful slopped over his neck and his embroidered vest. She rescued the glass — a pity to let it get broken. Then with infinitely gentle touch she turned back one of his eyelids. The eyeball showed white. He was deeply unconscious. She arranged his head comfortably on the cushion, sprinkled some more of the liqueur over him — not without regret at the waste — and, still as lightly as a hovering insect, drew the great signet-ring from his finger, and placed it on her thumb.

Then she made speed. The guard outside the outermost door let her through when he saw the ring. "Do not disturb your master," she said.

She had familiarised herself with the layout of the castle, and found her way quickly, yet with no show of haste, to the prison quarter. She spoke to the guard there, showing him the ring on her hand. He saluted it with a profound salaam.

"By order of your master, Raschid ed Din Sinan, and under his seal, you are to release the prisoner Fitzurse, and provide two fleet horses for him and for me, and escort us as far as the Well of Ishmael — and there leave us. In this you are not to fail." Once again she repeated a certain holy word.

It was soon done. Young Fitzurse, dazed and blinking in the light, found himself led out and placed on a horse, by the side of an astonishing white-robed nun, whom the Saracen guard, formidable though he was, treated with much deference.

At the Well of Ishmael, a landmark from which the Abbess knew she could find her way, she called a halt, and handed the ring back to the guard.

"Give this to your master," she said, thinking of how his servants would find him, smelling, not of hashish, but all too plainly of strong alcohol. "With my thanks. Tell him that a wise man who has lost a forbidden game, will not make too great an outcry against the winner. Oh, and tell him if his head aches, to try a strong draught of the 'kafiye' drink."

VII.
LITTLE
SILAS _____

The sisters of the convent of the Holy Alabastron at
Bethany were wont to take their daily recreation in
their beautiful enclosed garden, where the high
walls sheltered the palms and lilies from the drought
of summer and the cold winds of winter. A wicket
gate that opened upon the street without, was carefully kept by a lay-sister. Here, as the sisters were
soberly walking in the garden-paths, came the huntsman William ("videlicet 'Bil,'" as he appeared on the
convent's payroll) and handed something in a basket
to the portress. She carried it rather hesitantly to the
Abbess, the Lady Jovetta, who was entertaining her
guest and sister-Abbess, the Lady Hodierna of
Shaston. The black thick gown of the Alabastron
contrasted with the clean white of the Shaston.

"He says it's a strange beast he has found, Reverend Mother," said the portress. "But quite harmless
and indeed very young."

The Abbess Jovetta frowned and drew back a
little, but the Abbess Hodierna sprang up and ran
forward, crying, "Oh, let us see it!"

William videlicet Bil stood doubtfully at the
wicket, not sure if he would be told to take his gift
away again. The portress set the basket down and

cautiously removed the lid. All the nuns drew round in a circle, eagerly looking. They could see a small black curly head, and a pinky-brown back with a pencil-thin line of hair running down the spine; what looked like dimpled elbows doubled up, as if the little creature had its hands over its eyes. It might have been a human baby, though small even for a newborn one. But it looked almost as if there were two creatures there — a bunch of furry limbs, folded up, with a tiny hoof showing like a gazelle's. "Oh, it's a darling!" Hodierna exclaimed, and stooped to pick it up. A gasp came from the assembled nuns. There was a cherubic little human face, the eyes tightly screwed up, the soft rounded arms of a human baby, and the little human body down to the middle — and there, where one looked for legs, why, the small furry haunches of an animal, and the tiniest, neatest hooves ever seen.

With a slight exclamation of surprise, Hodierna laid it back in its basket.

"Oh, what is it?" cried the nuns.

"Why, I think it must be a child of the Satyrs," said Hodierna. "The wild men, out in the farthest wilderness."

"It can't be holy," said Jovetta. "It looks like the accursed offspring of an unnatural union between man and beast." She drew her veil across her face, shuddered, and crossed herself.

"No, that's not possible," said Hodierna. "Those wild men are a breed of their own. I've read of them.

The desert fathers used to meet them, though I never heard of any females. But the old books speak of the little Fauns, and the heathens used to paint and carve them. This must be one such." She bent down to it again. The little creature opened brilliant black eyes, and stared at her.

"Oh, he's a love!" cried young Sister Angelica.

"He stinks," said the Abbess Jovetta.

"He can be washed," said the Abbess Hodierna, and gathered him up in her arms. Sister Martha came running with a towel to place between the Abbess's spotless habit and the little heathen body.

"But can he be baptised?" said the Abbess Jovetta.

"Why not? He *looks* as if he had a soul."

"He looks like half a beast to me."

"Even if he's only half a soul, bring me some water from the fountain." The nuns brought a garden pitcher. "I'll call him Silas. That's videlicet Sylvanus, and means a wild man of the woods. And I'll be his godmother myself if no one else will be."

"My dear Shaston, I don't like it. You don't know what dangers there might be."

"My dear Alabastron, I'll take the risk. Here," and she stood up straight and tall in her white robe, looking strangely like a Madonna with the little hairy goat-legged Faun in her arms. "Silas, I baptise thee in the Name of the Father and of the Son and of the Holy Ghost, Amen."

She sprinkled the water, and made the cross, and the nuns said Amen. No sparks flew nor brimstone fumed. But the baby Faun began to cry, and Hodierna rocked him in her arms and comforted him.

"I suppose he'll have to have some clothes," said the Abbess Jovetta.

Silas, howling loudly, was duly bathed, and clothed in one of the little shirts the good sisters made in quantity for the children of the poor. It wasn't easy to make him keep it on. Still, as long as he lay in his basket, it was possible to keep him fairly decent under linen sheets. A nurse had to be found for him. Fortunately, one of the convent's habitual objects of charity was available — a Flemish girl, a camp-follower, who was certainly no better than she ought to be, but rather too stupid to be afraid of the strange creature, and as she had lost her own baby, she had abundance of milk, and was glad enough to nurse the little savage.

"That creature can't be anything good," the Abbess Jovetta insisted. "Look at his hooves. Like a goat's or the devil's."

"More like a sheep," retorted Hodierna, "or a lamb," with an upward glance at an Angus Dei in the chapel window, complete with golden hooves. Jovetta could say no more. Hodierna did not think it wise to mention to her that when she caressed the little fellow's curly head she could feel two hard knobs over the brows which grew larger every day.

Silas grew much more quickly than an ordinary baby. He did not need his wet-nurse for long. At about two months (though of course nobody knew his actual date of birth) he had sharp little teeth, and was eating solid food voraciously. The poor nurse was soon glad to be rid of him, for he bit her unmercifully. At three months he began to run about. It then became absolutely necessary for him to be clothed, to avoid scandal in the convent; for although his own hair, growing thick and long, covered his body from the navel down, it failed in certain important respects. This could not be allowed in a convent. A pair of breeches, at least, must be insisted on. But here he was excessively difficult, tearing off every pair of breeches they tried to put on him, and trampling them with his shiny little hooves. At last Hodierna hit on an answer. There was a perfume she used for her body-linen, mostly lavender, rosemary and pine. Silas knew it well. The next pair of breeches they tried on him was perfumed strongly with this spiced essence. Silas accepted the garment as a sign of her presence and her love.

For the strange little being adored her. She had always been closer to him than the wet-nurse; to her, he was a much more intelligent and satisfying companion than any dog or cat; to him, she was his goddess.

At a year old or thereabouts, he was as developed as a human child of four or five, and the little horns on his forehead were peeping through his curly hair, like points of onyx, to match his dainty onyx hooves. He was slow in learning to speak, though he seemed to understand all that was said to him — if he chose. For the older he grew, the more mischievous. A monkey, a teething puppy, a jackdaw, were nothing to him. Nothing that he could reach was safe from him, and his agility and dexterity were amazing. He would catch the little lizards that flickered on the wall, and to the dismay of both Abbesses, eat them. That was bad enough, but worse when he started to do the same with the day-old chicks in the poultry-yard. Unlike the lizards, the chicks were clean meat. But they were the convent's property. Hodierna whipped him for killing the chicks (no one else was allowed to lay a hand on him), but left him a free hand with the lizards, so long as he didn't eat them in her presence. She strongly suspected him of eating sparrows, too, and mice. As to rats, she hoped not, but thought it best not to enquire.

When he took to breaking out at night and wandering the countryside, she grew afraid of losing him: not only that he might try to get back to his own people, wherever they were, but because there were dangers outside — lions, jackals and hyenas. And, tough and resourceful though he was, he was still only a baby. So the little cell in which he slept, close to Hodierna, was fortified with bars and locked with a padlock at night. He cried at first, but when she came and talked to him, caressed him, loved him, and settled him in his little nest of straw and sheep-skins, he accepted it, so long as she never failed to bed him down for the night. He wore a little shirt and breeches; and came to chapel with her, crouching on the floor when the others knelt, mouthing the prayers, though nobody could be sure how much he under-stood. She gave him a little rosary, and he slipped the beads through his fingers with great pleasure, al-though Hodierna was very much afraid he made no sense of the prayers that should go with them. Still, she persevered with him, in spite of his great un-popularity throughout the convent.

Now a problem arose. The Abbess of Shaston had been away from her own convent for more than a year, and even she, whose word was her own law, could not absent herself forever. Her convent needed her, and before long she would have to leave Outremer and go back to England. What then would become of Silas?

"Let him go," urged Jovetta. "Send him back to the wilderness where he belongs. He should not be here."

"Send him back? But how? I can't turn him loose into the wild. He would die. The wild beasts would have him." She gathered him into her arms, feeling his little body palpitating through the coarse linen. "I'll never do that. And as for his own people — where are they? Huntsman Bil says they haven't been seen round here for years. They live away down in the deserts of Edom, or the other side of Galilee in the country of the Gergasenes, and no one ever sees them. Some say they have died out altogether."

"The other huntsman, Jacques," put in Sister Martha, "told the portress he thought he saw one of them last full moon, up on the hill there looking down on us."

"The Lord preserve us!" said Jovetta. "Looking down on us?"

"But when he searched he found nothing. He thinks it might have been only shadows, or some other beast."

"Heaven send it's so!" said Jovetta. "Tell him he must keep a more careful watch. And you'll make sure," she turned to Hodierna, "— that the — the child is safely locked up at night?"

Hodierna smiled and gathered him into her arms.

When the Abbess Hodierna spoke of returning to England, the Abbess Jovetta said nothing to dissuade her. Close friends and close kindred though they were, the Abbess of the Alabastron would have been infinitely glad to know that her unaccountable, unpredictable and altogether disquieting guest was safely back in her own convent.

Not the least of her worries was the Abbess Hodierna's disconcerting love of being alone. She would ride out into the countryside on a tall swift horse, accompanied only by one sister, and sometimes be out all day and until dangerously near sunset. Sometimes she took "that brat," the Satyr-boy, with her, for he could now keep up easily on foot with any horse; and if she did not take him, Bil the huntsman would have to shut him up till she was well out of sight, and lock him into his cell if she was late in returning, so that he could not rush out to look for her. It was all a great anxiety to Abbess Jovetta.

One day Silas had been especially naughty, so Hodierna had left him behind, though not without sharp words with Jovetta. In fact it was undoubtedly because of her smouldering wrath with her sister Abbess that Hodierna rode far, far out into the wilderness, in spite of the mild protests of Sister Salome, who accompanied her. Sister Salome was a good rider, and liked the wilderness, but she often felt that the Abbess went too far for too long; and this time she thought the Abbess would never turn back. The ground was all stony ridges, baking in the sun, grown over here and there with grim aloes and cactus, and that glimmering blue thorn that at a distance looks like bluebells in an English wood, until you approach it and find that the blue is only the colour of the cruel thorns. But the air was clear though warm, and the hills stretched away, and the sky was uplifting to the heart. The horses seemed to feel the freedom, the pleasure. At last with reluctance the Abbess turned toward home. The sun was sinking, and she enjoyed watching the beauty of the sunset.

Suddenly came a sound, a deep grunt, a kind of cough; both the horses started, reared, plunged. Before she could think Hodierna was flung to the ground. She struck her head against a stone, and lost consciousness. Sister Salome clung desperately to her saddle, as her terrified horse galloped, out of all control, away from the lion that bounded after it. Away and away, with Sister Salome helpless and shrieking. But the lion, lazier than a lioness would have been, tired of the chase, dropped behind and gave up; and Sister Salome's horse, running blindly, rushed her into the midst of a Bedouin village. Here she found herself a prisoner, but kindly treated, so that it was many days before she was able to return to the convent with news of the Abbess's fate.

And what had been her fate? When she regained consciousness, she looked about her, and found that it was dark night. Painfully she tried to rise, but felt so desperately full of pain that she sank down again. She felt as if her shoulder was broken. One ankle was badly twisted, but not broken as far as she could tell. Her head ached and buzzed; she felt sick and faint and desperately thirsty. She lay back as she had fallen and tried to gather her strength and consider what to do.

The thing that brought her onto her feet was the thin whine of an animal. Hyenas! She had guessed about the lion, in the split second before her head struck the stone; but this was worse. Lions were cowardly (in spite of the legends) and lazy, and could be driven off; but hyenas were resolute, and would track a man for days. Aware of her peril, she dragged herself to the side of a large boulder, and pulled herself to her feet by holding on to it.

Her eyes had adjusted themselves to the darkness now; the stars gave light. She could see the outlines of the rocky hills around her, but they meant nothing to her. Without much hope, she raised her voice and called Sister Salome; the desert echoes mocked her: "Salome! Salo-o-me! Salo-o-o-me!" No sound even of a horse. Perhaps the lion had killed Sister Salome, and her horse as well . . . She listened carefully, but heard not a hoofbeat, not a jingle, not a clink, only that thin howling again. And then she saw the dark, humpbacked shape of the beast, and its glittering eyes.

She knew the spells that controlled wild beasts, and others that controlled Air, Earth, Fire, and Water; but not one spell of all these could she remember. And the power and energy, which control the true magic, was so dim within her that she knew it would be useless for her to try to use them even if she could remember.

Wounded and in pain, thirsty, exhausted, fright-ened, there in the darkness she did what no one had ever seen her do — she sank down and cried. Cried helplessly, weakly, ready to give up altogether. No one to witness her humiliation. That was well. But, indeed, it was the awful solitude that crushed her, drained her of all power to go on living.

She might have died of exhaustion, but danger jolted her back. The hyena had crept up closer, in the dark, and was standing hardly more than an arm's length away from her, near her right shoulder. In the faint starlight she saw its small, mean face below hunched back — the red eyes, the sharp gleaming teeth . . . The brute was growling, and coming stiff-legged toward her. In spite of the pain in her shoul-der, she dragged herself upright again, holding on to the rock. There was just one small bit of magic she still could do, an elementary trick. Within reach of her hand was a small thornbush. She darted her fingers at it and put out her last spurt of energy. The bush burst into flame. The hyena cowered back, then turned and trotted away into the darkness. So far, a breathing space.

She still wore her riding gauntlets, and with their protection she managed to drag a few more thorn-bushes together, and build up a tolerable fire. Then, the excitement of the moment spent, she sank down again and considered her plight. She judged that her collar-bone was broken. She had gained some knowl-edge of such things when she nursed the wounded

Crusaders. The first thing to do was to tear her useless veil into strips and tie up her shoulder, though how to do it with one hand was a challenge. But manage it she did, and bandaged her ankle too. And then there was nothing to do but wait, and pray.

After a sleepless night she saw the sun come up and, looking round her, knew that she was far away from any known landmark, and completely lost. Perhaps the horse had dragged her in its panic, or perhaps she had already gone beyond her familiar landmarks when she fell. She had no idea where she might be. But at least the hyenas would not prowl by daylight. She dozed off, sitting against the rock with the ashes of her fire before her. Suddenly she woke, feeling something waving past her face and saw the hideous face of a vulture looking right at her. The shriek she gave scared it off. It lurched away clumsily and flapped into the air, as did two others behind it. Now she was afraid to sleep. Then the flies found her and tormented her. She was thirsty beyond all imagining. The sun beat down on her and seemed to grind her into the ground.

Then she began to hear grunts and whistles and heavy thumps on the ground, and bird-like chatterings; and opening her burning eyes, she saw that she was surrounded by creatures — men, were they? Bundles of black fur and grey hair was what they seemed to be at first, crowding and bobbing together, and emitting sounds that did not seem like any human language, but in the middle of the bundles of fur she seemed to see some human faces. Men of a sort, with long rough hair, crowned with what looked like horns; naked to the waist, and thence downward thickly covered with tangled black fur; and below that, unmistakably, goats' legs. She remembered little Silas. They had human faces certainly, and they did not look unfriendly. They were pressing round her like curious cattle. Without attempting to rise, she stretched out her hands to them in a gesture of appeal.

"Good people, help me!" she said. They might not understand her words, but her tone of voice might convey something.

She heard them all give a kind of sigh, and they bobbed their heads together in groups of three or four. As they turned, she could see that they had bristling tails like goats, wagging with excitement.

Then one came forward from the group, a youngish male, with quite a pleasant face.

"Me speak English," he said. "Ave Maria, pater noster, how-do-you-do?"

Weak and in pain though she was, the Abbess could hardly keep from laughing. This creature must have been a monastery servant, or a knight's retainer. But, thank heaven, here was an interpreter of a sort. In the simplest possible words she made known her plight to him, and he explained to the others. At once they were all sympathy and hurried to care for her. One brought a water bottle and gave her a drink. They examined her shoulder and her ankle, but she gave them very firmly to understand that they must let them alone. Then two of the largest of the wild men linked their hands and made a carrying-chair for her, and so bore her off to their encampment.

This was a cave, hardly more than a vertical crack in the rock of a mountainside, narrow and high, floored with sand. There was a small smoky fire, tended by two old female satyrs. One could hardly say that the place was furnished, but things were lying about that belonged to human occupation — sheepskins and goatskins, various rusty metal objects, a number of horns (probably their own, periodically dropped) roughly shaped into implements, and an appalling amount of rubbish and mess. The satyrs laid the Abbess gently and carefully on the sand floor, and made her as comfortable as they could with sheepskin rugs. The females brought her broth in a horn vessel. It was horrible stuff, and made of heaven knew what, but the Abbess was so thirsty and famished that she gulped it down without asking questions, like an old campaigner. They also brought her locusts, fried on a round bronze disc that seemed to have been a Saracen's shield. She ate them, remembering that St John the Baptist had done the same. She noticed also that the metal pot which simmered over their fire appeared to be the flat-topped helmet of a Templar.

There were about a dozen or fifteen of the satyrs, mostly males, but there were females — two grizzled and old, and five young, comely little creatures, with big bright eyes, pointed chins, leaf-shaped ears pointing up into curly black hair, dainty small horns curled like sheep's horns in spirals, and firm brown breasts. And running round the entrance of the cave were three or four tiny fauns, all very like Silas, playing and scuffling and dancing. Should she tell them about Silas? She could not be quite sure, and "when in doubt, don't" was always good counsel.

At sunset the tribe went to bed. They huddled together on the sandy floor in the depths of the cave, in a tight furry heap, buried in each other's hair, snorting and snuffling and palpitating like a litter of puppies. To show their great consideration for the Abbess, they placed her in the centre of the pile. She wrapped her clothes as tightly round her as possible, with the remnants of her veil swathed round her head and eyes, and accepted the situation. There may have been some soporific herb in the broth they gave her, for in spite of everything she dropped suddenly off to sleep, and slept well. But on waking, with the tribe lifting off her one by one until she could stagger up, she found herself bitten by fleas from head to foot. In the manner of her time, nobody minded a few civilised fleas, but this was beyond measure. Her dismayed exclamation, as the dim light of morning came into the cave, brought the two old females, who clicked their tongues anxiously, and brought a horn full of some sticky, odorous stuff, which they rubbed all over her. It soothed the bites, and seemed to repel any further fleas.

She was reasonably well, all things considered, but very weak and tired. After a breakfast of more locusts (she would have preferred some wild honey!) she sat at the mouth of the cave in the sun, while most of the adult males prepared to go off in their endless search for food.

"Will you take me home now?" she said to her interpreter, whose name seemed to be something like "Kraa." "My home is Bethany," she ventured, wondering how to explain to him, and indeed having no idea in what direction it lay.

"Savvy you home," he replied. "Black ladies, white faces, Domus-Dei . . . savvy Bethany. Take you there, but not yet."

"But why not?"

"Nondum allee, ex-pec-ta-moos Mother Acha."

"Oh, and who is Mother Acha?"

"Acha — Mother. Lose her baby. Black ladies take her baby. Steal, bad. Her allee regardee for baby. Regardee all time Domus Dei. We no allee till she come."

The Abbess's heart smote her. Silas! But still she thought it better to say nothing.

All that day she remained with the satyrs, and that night, sharing their peculiar life. They were gentle, courteous, and considerate to her, and gave her all the comforts they had to give.

Then on the morning of the next day, suddenly the expected one arrived. Mother Acha.

She was a formidable creature. Much taller and larger than any of the other satyrs, even the males, and covered nearly all over with black hair, except where her pink globular breasts thrust through; instead of the small leaf-shaped ears of the others, she had long upright tubular ears like a cow's, between which thrust her horns, long and pointed like a buffalo's. A great bunch of grizzled hair brushed her forehead, and two other great bunches hung behind her ears. Her face would have been hard and repellent even in a human. In her hand she held a long staff tipped with a pair of horns — goat's or satyr's horns. Seen so, black against the rising sun, she was as complete a picture of a devil risen from the pit of hell as even the Abbess could imagine.

But the Abbess kept her head. These creatures were flesh and blood, and this was no demon, only an ugly, angry mother. But possibly she would have found a real evil spirit easier to deal with.

The she-satyr advanced upon her, pointing two fingers forkwise. She spoke vehemently in their strange language.

"Tell me what she says," she asked Kraa. "And tell her to put those fingers down, or I will curse her also."

"She say," he interpreted, "you are the Black Lady took her baby."

The other satyrs murmured with shock.

"I don't deny it," said the Abbess. "Tell her, yes, I took her baby, but I will give him back."

"She say you put him clothes."

The Abbess smiled. "Yes, of course I put him clothes."

The satyr murmured again.

"She say, you make him Christian."

"Oh yes," smiling again, and gesturing with benevolence toward the crowd. "I make him Christian. Make you all Christian?"

This was met with frowns and stamping of hooves.

"She say, you make him priest."

This time the Abbess laughed. "No, no! Not Silas! No, he couldn't ever be that."

"She say, you make him eunuch!"

A deep growl came from the crowd.

"Oh, no!" cried the Abbess. "God forbid! Tell her I would never, never do any such thing . . ."

With gesture and expression, she tried all she knew to convince them of her abhorrence of such an idea.

"Tell her," she said, "I will give him back to her at once, whole and unharmed. Yes, at once, willingly."

As the translated reply was understood, the tension relaxed. Acha lowered her pitchfork, drooped her shoulders, turned aside as an animal will when a struggle for supremacy is yielded, but then came back.

"She says, when you give back?"

"Now, today. But she must come with me to Domus Dei."

Murmurs of dismay and disapproval.

"She say no allee Domus Dei. Us nunquam allee there. Bad for us. You bring him here."

"Bring him here? But how?"

"You call him. He come."

The Abbess gasped with astonishment — that these people should believe so simply that she could call him, could exert a spiritual pull on him at that distance. It seemed they recognised the power that she had and were asking her, in all confidence, to use it. But could she? She still felt weak and drained of psychic strength, as well as being without any of the apparatus that helps a magician, without even a book in case her memory was faulty. All must depend on her sheer power of psychic attraction, if only it were strong enough. And what of the poor child himself?

"But it's a long way for him to come," she said. "Too far. You can't expect him to come all that way alone. Poor little child, he'd die in the wilderness."

Acha seemed to understand this.

The interpreter said, "She say, we allee so proxim we can Domus Dei. Than you call him." So it was agreed.

It was a long day's march over the hot sand and riven rocks. Then at last they came in sight of the hills of

Bethany and could see far off the convent of the Alabastron, on the edge of the town, its white walls facing the wilderness. The satyr tribe halted on the ridge of hills.

"Now you call him," said the interpreter.

"I'll use what arts I can," said the Abbess. "But I must have a place alone to myself, day and night. I will not run away, but you may guard me if you want to."

In that country of caves it was not hard to find a small cave that was reasonably suitable, facing south. The sun illumined it most of the day, and at night the Abbess had a fire to herself, and some sheepskin rugs, verminous though they were, against the sudden chill of the night. She drew the appropriate circles on the smooth sand inside the cave. A young satyr mounted guard a hundred paces outside.

Here she tried, in the blessed quiet, to gather her powers by meditation and mental exercise, and also by prayer. And then, it being early afternoon, she put her powers to the test, picturing the image of young Silas, uttering toward him the Word of Command over the creatures of the earth, and then reaching out to him, calling, pulling him toward her. And the satyrs, assembled on the hill's crest, waited in confidence, watching the walls of the convent, and the road that led therefrom . . . but no one came.

Meanwhile, in the convent of the Alabastron, the nuns, already mourning the loss of Mother Hodierna, were flung into a state of terror once again. Mother Jovetta, having noticed how young Silas moped and wandered, looking everywhere for Hodierna, carefully shut all doors and windows in the daytime and secured him in his cell at night. Now the silence of the midday rest was wrecked by his high-pitched howling, as he struggled at one door after another. He was like a mad thing. With the help of Bil, Jovetta got him into his cell and locked the door. Here he continued to wail and struggle.

The satyrs, away on the hill, crowded round the entrance to Hodierna's cave. Acha stood over her, threatening. "You bring him, or I kill you." The words she uttered hardly needed interpreting.

The Abbess shook her head, spread her hands.

"Tell them," she told Kraa, "I do what I can. Let me go on. He will come soon."

The next night when she was alone, she tried again, but still with no success. Now, as her subtle perceptions reached out, she sensed two things. She was convinced that she had made contact with Silas, whose open intuitive nature, more sensitive even than a primitive man's, because it was partly an animal's, yearned and struggled to come to her, and, secondly, that another will withstood him, a watchful and steely will . . . Jovetta's.

She sharpened and drove her perception to the point where she could see. There was Silas, forlornly crouched in his cell behind bars, and there, outside, sat Jovetta, keeping vigil all night, unsleeping, with the key of the cell at her girdle.

Hodierna suddenly perceived that Jovetta could see her. To Jovetta she was a white ghostly gleaming in the dark corridor, a presence that did not go away when she made the sign of the cross at it.

"Pax tecum, my dear Mother Jovetta."

"You! They told me you were dead . . . if it *is* you."

"But here I am. Give up the boy, Jovetta. He must go back to his people. Take that key and unlock his door."

"No." Just plain and uncompromising. No more words to be said. Hodierna felt that her power was spent. She faded from Jovetta's sight and was back, exhausted, in her cave.

One more evening, sunset. "You no get him, me grand peur they kill you," said Kraa.

"Oh, I'll try again. But they must go away." She set herself to the struggle once more. She must save her powers, she knew. No use to appear to Jovetta again. She must direct all her energy now to swaying Jovetta's mind.

Her searching thought made contact with Jovetta's and projected into it a straight command: unlock that door. But Jovetta's mind resisted and could not be overcome. Fear? No image of fear could shake that stony composure. Appeal to pity? There was no pity there. Jovetta's mind was armoured in cold steel. No weak spot? Yes, Hodierna remembered. One weak spot: memory. From Hodierna's mind into Jovetta's there flashed the image of a face — pale, dark-eyed, Asiatic. Emotion broke into Jovetta's heart. At once all her will was softened, her conscious mind was blinded. Without knowing what she did, her hand went to the key, and the key to the lock. Silas was out and running. Something said to Jovetta, as in a sleep-walker's ear, "Open the back door and let him out." She did so. On his dancing, clicking hooves he pattered across the stony ground, and Jovetta felt herself drawn back to her own cell and lay on her bed to sleep, till the convent bell woke her to sudden panic.

But Hodierna, drawing a long breath of relief, saw the distant, tiny shape of the faun running toward her in the moonlight. The satyrs, lying in a ring a hundred paces away from her, leapt up as she approached them.

"Look!" she called out. "He comes!"

He was indeed coming, rapidly making his way up the slope below them. The Abbess, with Acha by her side, stood in front of the crowd. He reached them.

"Mother!" he cried, and held out his arms to the Abbess.

There was no need to translate the fierce exclamation that broke from Acha's lips, as she grabbed Silas's arm and swung him toward her.

"*I* am his mother, not you!"

Eyes blazing, hair bristling, she charged head downward at the Abbess, one sharp horn directed straight at her breast.

With a shriek, Silas rushed between them, and seizing both horns, flung himself across Acha's face, so that she swerved, trying to shake him off. In that moment Hodierna found her magical energy returned to her. A flash of light held everyone spellbound like statues for an instant, just as they were. Then slowly they returned to animation. The moment of fury had passed. The crowd sighed deeply. The satyress drooped her heavy head, and the little faun loosed his hold of her horns and slid to the ground. She took him in her arms.

"Listen," the Abbess said, loud and clear. "You, Kraa, tell them. This child is yours, Acha. Take him. Silas, my darling, you must stay with your mother now. God bless you all." Without another word, without a backward glance, she walked past them, and down the long road to the distant convent. The satyrs drew together, gathering Silas into their midst as a flock of apes would have done. She thought she heard him crying, but she did not look back to see whether he was content with his lot. She knew she must not. But oh, she thought, the different life which she had given him. He, who had known nothing but the gentle propriety and civilised comforts of the convent, to sleep in verminous sheepskins and range the desert for locusts. . . .

She reached the convent porch, and pulled the bell.

The convent buzzed like a disturbed hive.

"I thought — they told me you were dead," said Jovetta.

"But here I am." Both had a strange sense of having said the same words before.

"Silas is missing," said Jovetta.

"I know. He has gone back to his own people, as he should. Look!" She pointed to where, on the brow of the hill in the moonlight, the dark, furry crowd of satyrs could be seen. "He is there with them, with his own mother. Leave him alone. Let good food be left for them, as much as we can spare. Let it be left a mile away from the walls, and let nobody watch for them. But we must not see Silas again."

She went slowly back to her own quarters, and later, when she was alone, she wept a little once more. But whether her tears were for Silas because of his new hard life, or for herself, because she had lost him, is not known. Indeed whether she herself had ever known the pains and joys of motherhood will never be known.

VIII.
MARDUK ─────────────────

It sometimes happened, and is recorded in history, that the warring hosts of the Crusaders and the Saracens agreed upon a truce and rested from their warfare, even their commanders taking sweet sherbet together in the privacy of their headquarters, and both sides meeting together as human beings. But those zealots, the Templars and the Hospitallers, saw to it that this never lasted long.

It was one of these happy interludes, in fine mild weather, on the outskirts of Jerusalem. By mutual agreement the cleared ground outside the fortifications had been opened to all, and made to look festive with banners; and the silk-robed Saracen officers, and the Christian knights in velvets instead of chain-mail, walked to and fro together, talking with friendly sympathy of what both sides had to endure, and hoping perhaps for a lasting settlement. The Frankish ladies were there, in their finest robes, admiring the formidable Eastern fighters, but the Saracen ladies were conspicuous by their absence, though everyone knew that they were there in the city, keeping close by themselves in their luxurious if temporary quarters.

The Abbess of Shaston was there, walking to and fro, one of a group of four, for less than that was considered indiscreet. Not that the Abbess cared, but she was not on her home ground; she was once again a guest of the Abbess Jovetta of the Convent of the Holy Alabastron on the road to Bethany. The Abbess Jovetta and her nuns were of the strict Benedictine rule, and she, with her attendant nun, wore their severe black, even in that sunshine; but Abbess Hodierna, of Shaston, on her left hand, with Sister Ruth beside her, met the sunshine in the white and blue of the Order of Saint Evodias and Saint Syntyche, an Order about which Jovetta was rather doubtful.

She turned to her guest.

"Pardon, my dear Hodierna. I must leave you now, to return to my duties. To tell the truth, I do not greatly like these occasions."

"Oh, don't put yourself out for us," said Hodierna. "Ruth and I will be well enough here. We quite enjoy it."

One of the knights stepped forward. "Oh, Lady Abbess, have no fear. I'll look after these ladies."

"Thank you. Farewell for now, dear Shaston, and don't get into more mischief than you can help."

As she turned away, the Abbess Hodierna said to the knight, "Who is that magnificent Saracen noble there, with the blazing jewel on his breast? He keeps on looking toward us."

"Oh, that is Messire Haroun-bin-Ishak, a well-known commander in the wars — kinsman of Saladin himself. Shall I present him to you?"

"Pray do so," said Hodierna.

Their new acquaintance made the sweeping gesture of reverential greeting, and then bent low over the Abbess's hand. The knight withdrew.

"Madame," said the Saracen, using the French form. "I have long desired a word with you. I think you speak our language?"

"I do, a little," she replied in surprisingly fluent Aramaic. "Unless you would rather I spoke in French or in German?"

"Madame, as I foresaw, you are a marvel. But I have a request to make."

"Why, say on," she said, her candid blue eyes steadily upon him.

"My dear Madame, it is this: will you instruct me in your Christian faith? For I long to learn it."

If she felt any surprise, the Abbess did not show it.

"Why, I should be delighted, but why do you not ask one of our priests? We have many. Or even the bishop himself? It would be more suitable, and they are very wise."

"Ah, but, Madame, I am afraid of them. Your solemn priests, your great bishop, I dare not approach them."

"No, no," she smiled. "Why should you be afraid? They are kind men, and will not refuse you. They are good shepherds."

A tinge of colour seemed to run up from his trim beard over his cheeks.

"Madame, I tell you, I am afraid of them! But you, so gentle a shepherdess, would lead me so that I would not run away."

He seemed entirely sincere, and very human. A convert? How lovely that would be, and his people after him — why not? In the end she gave way.

"I will give you a letter to show at the gate," she said. "It will admit you to the little private garden at the back of the Convent of the Holy Alabastron. I am allowed to use that little garden, with my nuns, as my own. You may come there for one hour on Thursdays, which is neither our holy Sunday nor your holy Friday, for one hour only, between Nones and the next bell. I will be there, but of course not alone, but I will talk quietly to you and tell you of our belief." She wrote a discreet little note, and gave it to him, and so left him. She did not tell the other Abbess of the arrangement; it was not really her affair. Hodierna had been told to use that little garden as her own.

It was a charming little garden, high walled, and carefully watered from its own well. Grass had been laid down there and nurtured, and a few large palms and flowering shrubs, and many rose trees, and tall lilies in their cool corners. Here of an afternoon Hodierna sat in a comfortable basketwork chair in the shadiest spot, with rose trees behind her and turf under her feet; and here on Thursdays after Nones, Sister Ruth led in Haroun-bin-Ishak, and placed a low stool for him at the Abbess's side and a pile of books on the table, and left him, but she did not go far. On the other side of a great clump of palms and shrubs, Sister Ruth had a chair, and there she sat, out of sight, quietly, with her needlework. When the convent bell struck the hour, she led him discreetly out again.

The Abbess found him an intelligent pupil. She delighted to expound her faith to him, a faith full of sunshine and fresh air. Sometimes they discussed his own religion, and others, the strange beliefs of the East — fate, and the stars, and all manner of wonders — and of creation, and beauty, and love. She found it refreshing to exchange ideas with one unfettered by her own conventions. So it went on for six successive Thursdays.

"You speak of love," he said, "of the holy love of God, and of the soul that yearns to God; of the love of all creation, and of the beauty of even one rose, which is here made visible; and of the love of blessed souls for one another. But is there nothing of the love of man and woman?"

She coloured a little, and began to pack her books together.

"I think," she said, "I have taught you all that I can. You should now go to the learned Canon De la Croix. I will give you a letter to him. I do not think you need come to me again."

He rose from his low stool.

"Oh, but Madame, do you mean that we must say good-bye?"

"Yes," she said very firmly, but with perhaps a touch of regret. "Sister Ruth."

Three days after he had left her, when she was beginning to feel that life was very dull, a little girl messenger was brought to her. A slim little thing, perhaps twelve years old, richly dressed in turquoise-blue silk. She made the usual deep salaam.

"Madame Abbess," she said, "I bring a message from the Lady Zara, the wife of the honoured Haroun-bin-Ishak."

She spoke in French, but from the words she used, the Abbess understood that "the wife" meant the chief wife of many, the queen of the household.

"My mistress tells me to beg you of your kindness to come tomorrow and visit her in her dwelling close within the walls of the city, to drink sherbet and spend a pleasant hour with her. My mistress desires it greatly. Madame, will you come?"

The Abbess considered. She asked the other Abbess. Jovetta shook her head. "It might be a trap," she said.

"But why should it be? We are at peace with the Saracens now." (There was more that she knew, but she did not share her knowledge with the other Abbess.) "Everyone will know where I have gone, and it will be only for an hour. What harm could there be in it?"

"All sorts of harm," the other Abbess replied sourly. "But I suppose as usual you'll go."

That decided her. She told the little messenger that she would come. The girl said a litter would come and fetch her. After all, three or four ladies of the Crusaders' families had already visited some of the Saracen ladies in their little pavilions within the walls.

Next day Hodierna prepared with care, not only, as Jovetta grimly recommended, with prayer and holy water, but she put on her crispest white robes and finest linen veil, and her special rosary from her blue girdle. This was a thing of her own, the usual number of beads and so forth, but each of the large beads or "gaudies" was a different colour and pattern. She checked them over to see if they were all there.

The dwelling of Haroun-bin-Ishak was at some little distance, on the other side of Jerusalem, but the Abbess was conveyed there very comfortably in a litter carried by four large men, the little messenger girl running behind them. The residence seemed to be rather a complicated construction of sheds and shacks behind the fortifications, but one fine roof towered above the rest. Inside all was cool, comfortable, and elegant. The privations of a siege had not reached here; indeed it was only in later years that the rigour of siege warfare became known. It was evident that as soon as the truce was proclaimed every kind of amenity and pleasure had been quickly imported here. The Abbess was led along lighted corridors over soft carpets, and came to a roofed space that enclosed a large swimming bath, on the marble pavements of which pretty girls, in little or no garments, lay at ease. Overhead the sunlight came through softly coloured glass. Here the great lady herself came toward the Abbess.

The Lady Zara was a tall, shapely woman, her skin as white as the Abbess's own, her hair golden, and piled on her head with jewelled pins. She wore a length of flowing, many-coloured silk draped around her loins, and above that, only a rich array of ornaments. She advanced to the Abbess with the customary salutation and pressed both her hands.

"I am honoured by your visit," she said in excellent French. "Will you not lay aside your veil and your other garments, now we are private?"

The Abbess would have liked to throw off her cumbersome wrappings but felt unable to do such a thing. "Pardon me, Princess," she said, "but I may not do so. But it is cool here, is it not?"

Her eyes roved around the pleasant scene. The girls were playing with a monkey, an attractive little creature, his appealing little face framed in fluffy grey hair, his clever little hands going to and fro in a pantomime of his own. He was dressed in a poppy-red tunic of silk that reached to his knees; under it a pretty grey tail could be seen. He wore a poppy-red cap on his head.

"Marduk!" the lady called, and he left the girls and came running to her.

"This is Marduk," said the lady. "We are all very fond of him. Come and greet our visitor, Marduk."

The little fellow bowed to the ground in a sweeping "Salaam," and then took off his cap and flourished it in quite a French manner.

"Let us go into my special place," said Zara. She led the way to an alcove carved out of the great bathing hall, where arches, decorated with elaborate designs of flowers and creeping tendrils, enclosed a small, dainty fountain, springing from a basin of turquoise blue. Around the pool were low-padded seats piled with cushions in delicate colours. Zara led the Abbess to a very comfortable seat by the fountain's edge and sat beside her while an attendant brought them drinks.

The Abbess saw no reason to be suspicious, but a personal rule which she always kept when visiting totally strange places made her draw back.

"I am under a vow," she said. "Today I must not eat or drink until after sunset."

"Oh, what a pity!" said the lady. "Is it one of your saints' days?"

The Abbess thought quickly. The lady *might* know the important dates; swiftly she improvised one.

"Saint Mabelle," she said. "She fasted forty days until the drought was broken."

"Oh." The lady looked at her.

Zara's eyes were the deepest brown the Abbess had ever seen, large and very round. In vain the Abbess tried to read them. Nothing but childish wonder and contentment seemed to appear there. An attendant brought a tray of wonderful-looking sweetmeats, loucoum, and candied fruits. It was hard to resist them. But one thing Hodierna did not refuse. The lady selected from a tray of pretty things a really beautiful small enamel box, shaped like a drum. She carefully opened it.

"Take it home with you," she said, "and apply it to your lovely pale skin. The sun here is too fierce for white skins like yours and mine. This will soothe your face and neck and bosom. It is made from the juice of a very rare plant, which is found only in the regions south of Egypt, in the Mountains of the Moon. Take it and use it to preserve your beauty."

"Thank you very much," said the Abbess, and took it carefully in her hand. But the little monkey, who had been staying close to them and watching what they did, snatched it.

"No, no, Marduk, give it back," said the lady, in a tone of quiet command. But the monkey kept a hold on it, and skipped away.

"Marduk, Marduk!" The lady's voice rose to a scream of alarm. The monkey was clambering up the carving in the arch above them; he hopped out of reach to the next arch.

"Oh, Marduk, Marduk, no!" Far out of reach he settled on a branching tendril, facing a large round carved flower, as he had seen his mistress face her mirror at her dressing-table. He unfastened the box. The girls came running in; the lady screamed again.

The monkey dug his fingers into the pink ointment, took a handful, and smeared it on his face. Then his shrieks rose above the rest. He clapped his little hands to his eyes, shrieked again in agony, and, curling his body up helplessly, fell down on the pavement.

The lady stood transfixed. The girls surrounded the poor little thing, as he screamed, but more faintly, and rolled in convulsions.

The Abbess stepped forward, stripping off her veil and wrapping it round her hands. She grabbed the suffering creature in the folds of her veil, keeping the fabric between her hands and his frantic teeth and claws.

"Get warm water and cloths," she said to the girls. While they brought them she took one of the large beads of her rosary and unscrewed it. When the girls returned, she shook a little quantity of powder into the bowl of water. Then she began to pour the mixture over the poor monkey. Carefully she washed off the ointment as best she could and transferred him, now a little quieter, into another piece of linen. Only then did she turn to Zara.

"What is it?" she demanded abruptly. The lady, very pale, stammered out two words.

"Lilith's hair."

Immediately the Abbess took another of her beads and shook its contents into another bowl of water. When she bathed the monkey's face and paws in this, the convulsions ceased, and he seemed to fall asleep. Now the Abbess looked at Zara.

Zara had struggled to her feet, the girls aiding her.

"Oh, Madame. Oh, Madame, I can't — I can't . . . What can I say?"

"Say nothing," said the Abbess, steadily, though she was still trembling with shock. "Your poor Marduk will recover. He will even recover his sight after a time. I will tell your maids what to do for him. Yes, I know what it was meant for. You were jealous of me, you thought your husband — dear lady, it was never any such thing. He may have desired me — for a moment — but he got no help from me. And now, now you will not see me again, nor will he, for the truce is broken — it was the Templars and we must resume our war. I shall leave tonight."

The lady was crouching at her feet.

"Madame, yes, I was jealous, but I never thought . . . oh, my poor animal! And you, you came like an angel . . . and think what would have happened to you!"

"No, don't think," said the Abbess. "Get up, and help your maids to tend the poor creature. I will send someone with medicines for him before I leave."

The lady was covering her hands with kisses. Very quietly the women arranged the litter and found her a new silk veil; they washed her hands and set her on her way.

As she went the Abbess saw the stir in the camp and heard the shouts. As she had known some hours before, the truce was over.

IX.
CRUSADER
DAMOSEL _____

When Adela learnt that her father was to go to the
Holy Land, taking her and her mother with him, she
was delighted. Her mother, Dame Blanche, was less
delighted, but there was not much choice in the
matter. Sir Brian de Bassecourt, of Stoke Bassecourt
in the county of Kent, had been ordered by the
Abbot to go on the Crusade, or else build an expen-
sive chantry for the abbey — for Sir Brian had killed
a monk. He hadn't really meant to kill the monk, he
said, but when he found him halfway up the stairs to
Dame Blanche's bower, he had given him a little
push down, and the man had broken his neck. The
Abbot acquitted him of wilful murder, but gave him
the choice of the chantry or the Crusade. Sir Brian
wasn't a rich man: the Crusade might cost a good
deal of money, but the chantry would cost far more.
Besides, there were advantages, as he pointed out to
Dame Blanche.

"Just think — we get all our sins forgiven, all of
them — yours, too, and Adela's. And if we should die
on the journey —"

Dame Blanche gave a shriek.

"*If* we should, we'd all go to heaven at once. No
Purgatory at all. Think of that!"

"I'd rather not think of that," said Dame Blanche.

"Don't, then, my dear. Never mind. There're other things. Almost everyone who goes out to Outremer comes back with a fortune. There is plunder, and ransoms. There are even lands and castles for the picking up. *And* we'd be sure to find a husband for Adela, which is more than we'll do here."

So Dame Blanche went about her preparations, tearfully at first, and later with zeal and fervour. And Adela watched the preparations with mounting excitement.

Adela was fifteen, and had never been outside Stoke Bassecourt, where her family lived in a humdrum little farmhouse dignified by the name of Manor, which Duke William had bestowed on Sir Brian's great-grandfather. Adela had a fine Norman profile, jet-black hair, and blue eyes inherited from a Saxon grandmother. She was a bold girl, something of a tomboy, a good rider, and afraid of nothing she had ever encountered. But attractive as she was, she had little choice but to go into a convent and be done with it, in that dull little corner, where she'd never find a husband. After an overwhelming fuss and bother of preparation, they set out: Sir Brian in armour on his big charger, Dame Blanche in a mule litter, Adela on a palfrey. She had devised a dress for herself which was like the one created by Queen Eleanor some seventy years before, when she and all her ladies went on the First Crusade with King Louis, before she became Queen of England. Well-cut leather breeches, discreetly covered by a long, voluminous divided skirt, so full and flowing that no one could see that underneath all that brocade, the wearer was sitting easily astride a man's saddle. There was also a light corselet of soft leather, shaped to enhance the figure very discreetly, and covered with a silken surcoat. In that outfit, with a hooded cape for the rain, Adela sat proudly and confidently on her pretty black mare.

The first rallying point was at Wrotham, for the Kentish levies. Here the Crusaders made their vows and "took the Cross." Sir Brian had a bold red cross, made of two stripes of red cloth, stitched to his mantle, which he wore while he took the Crusader's Oath in the church.

Adela wanted to be enrolled as a Crusader too. She saw at least two imposing ladies going up and receiving the Cross. "Why can't I?" she asked Sir Brian. "*They* can."

"Oh, yes, dear, they do let ladies take the Cross, but only if they bring their own retinue of fighting men, as those two ladies are doing. I'm afraid my small following is barely a quota for one. Besides that, you are under age."

But the noble words of the Crusader's Oath stayed in Adela's mind and haunted her. She wove daydreams about riding out with a long sword at her side, to help King Guy to defend Jerusalem, fighting to keep the heathen from regaining the Holy Sepulchre, the most sacred spot on earth.

Somehow the milling crowd crossed the Channel. In the fields of France a long caravan formed, and slowly made its straggling way across Europe. It was an astonishing assembly: knights and noblemen with their soldiers; bands of volunteers from the country trudging with their bows; monks and clerics of every order; pilgrims, peddlers, hucksters, and sutlers; wives and families of fighting men — and, of course, a number of dubious ladies who travelled with the wagons and were discreetly known as "baggage." Then there were smiths and cooks, with their furnaces and cauldrons, and flocks of sheep and herds of cattle to provide meat on the hoof, and Lord-knows-what besides.

It was like a slowly moving town. Every day saw them strung out along the road, all in their accustomed order, with marshals riding up and down the line to keep them together. At night there could be the most astonishing variety of resting places. Sometimes they would reach a town or a castle, and then some of them at least (particularly the ladies, such as Adela and her mother) would be guests in comfort — or in more or less discomfort, as the luck was. Sometimes the company would halt in the open country, and make camp. Everyone would pitch his tent, and once you became accustomed to the routine, it wasn't bad at all. When a camp was made, it was a good opportunity to go up and down the lines and call on one's friends. Blanche did a good deal of visiting, with Adela beside her, rather overwhelmed with the newness of it all, and for the time being, diffident and a little withdrawn. Sir Brian brought young knights to their tent and presented them, ceremoniously, to Blanche and Adela. They were fine to look at, but Adela could find nothing to say to them.

Every morning began solemnly with Mass, either in the church of the town where they happened to be, or in a great pavilion set up with an altar and all the holy adornments — the knights and ladies devoutly kneeling on the grass outside. (Dame Blanche took care to bring a cushion.) One morning at a spot halfway through France, when Mass was being celebrated in the pavilion, and all the company was ranged in order outside, Adela looked over her right shoulder, and saw a phalanx of men, standing four-square together, in straight rows. All wore armour, and over the armour white tunics and long white mantles, emblazoned with the red cross. Their helmets were round, and cut straight across the top, like round towers. Something grim and resolute marked these men out from the rest. Adela looked at their faces, such of them as she could see. Mostly bearded, greyish, lined, some of them scarred. But one . . . he was young, bright-eyed. Something about him said to Adela: "This is the one."

She had turned half round, very daringly, and for the life of her she could not keep from fixing her eyes on his face. He looked at her for one moment — dark brown his eyes were — and a flash of understanding passed between them. Then Dame Blanche was pinching Adela's arm quite painfully, and jerking her round. Adela returned to her devotions. But she hardly knew what she was doing.

At the end of Mass, Adela stole a discreet glimpse over her shoulder. But now the crowd in general turned to see the men in white mantles, frowning and aloof, marching away in disciplined ranks. She tried in vain to see the face she had noticed.

"Adela," her mother said, "you mustn't look at those men. Don't you know who they are? Those are the Knights Templars."

"Are they? Well, what's wrong with them?"

"Nothing's *wrong* with them. But don't you understand, they mustn't look at women, or even let women look at them. They are under a vow of poverty, obedience, and — chastity. You keep your eyes away from them, dearest."

But Adela had already looked once too often.

The Templars, part of whose duty it was to protect those on their way to the Holy Land — pilgrims and relatives and dependents of Crusaders — now constituted themselves a guard to the company. Strung out at intervals, they patrolled the borders of the road, as well as the front and rear of the procession. They changed their positions often, and so one day Adela saw that face again, and then again, and learned from some of the servants that his name was Hugo Des Moulins, and that despite his French name, he was an English knight from Sussex. Twice she looked him in the face; the first time he responded with a kind of breathlessness, and the second time with a frown of anxiety, almost of pain. She knew she ought not to think about him, but how could she help it? As they continued on their way to Venice, and from there took ship (a dreadful passage it was) to Acre, she grew more and more desperate. At last, at Acre, as soon as they were settled into their humble quarters in the great stony fortress, she felt she must take action. When she learned where that lady's quarters were, she sought out the Abbess of Shaston.

Adela had heard that the Abbess was a remarkable woman, that she knew a wonderful great deal about a great many things: people came to her to be cured of illnesses, and of heartaches — to resolve doubts, and points of law, and settle quarrels; to seek love, or to be delivered from love; she was sought by women who wished to have babies, and, it was whispered, by those who did not. She could not be called a midwife nor a leech, for such occupations would be beneath the dignity of an Abbess; but it was thought that she knew more than all the wise-women and all the doctors together. She travelled to the

Holy Land and back as it pleased her, and it was said that she knew the secrets of the Saracens as well as of the Christians. She was certainly not a witch. Nobody dared say such a thing, for she had high connections. She obeyed no authority lower than the Pope's — if his, seeing that it was rumored that she was his cousin. Adela sought her out, taking with her the little jewel-box she always carried with her, containing such modest jewelry as she possessed. She opened the box, and left it lying open before the Abbess.

"Put those things away, child," said the Abbess. "Now tell me. You're in love, of course."

Adela told her.

"A Templar? That's difficult. Why did it have to be a Templar, you silly girl? You know he can't marry you. Do you want to be his paramour?"

Adela blushed. "Oh, but Templars don't have paramours."

"Don't they, then? There's a lot you don't know about Templars. But that wouldn't do for you, nor for him, I think. What do you want, then?"

"Can't a Templar ever be absolved from his vows?"

"Oh, yes, he can. The Pope can dispense his vow. I'd see it done myself. The Pope would do it for me." She spoke with airy assurance. "Only — the petition must come from the Templar, not from anyone else. He himself must ask for it. Would he do that — for you?"

"He doesn't know me," said Adela with her eyes downcast.

"No? Oh, but he does, though. He dreams of you."

"How . . . how on earth do you know?

"Never mind how, but I know. You and he know each other quite well, on the Other Side of the Curtain. But that's no good for earthly matters."

"What do you mean — the Other Side of the Curtain?"

"The other side of life and being. Even beyond dreams. Out of the body. You and he meet together, night after night, while your dreams hang a misleading curtain before your mortal minds."

Adela felt as if a great window was opened before her, full of beauty and wonder.

"Oh, if only I could know! If only I could remember! Could you not send me through the Curtain in my waking mind, or make it so that I can remember?"

"My child, I believe I could. But you must attend and do exactly as I say."

Then she gave Adela certain instructions, and taught her certain words and certain signs. Once again she waved aside Adela's jewel-box.

That night, Adela, lying on her bed wide awake, and having done all that the Abbess told her, felt herself rise out of her body, as a hand slips out of a glove. She looked down at herself, and went lightly out of doors, across the night and into a moonlit orchard, where Hugo was waiting for her.

"Welcome, my dear companion," he said, and clasped both her hands, but did not kiss her. It was enough for her — so far — just to feel his happy fellowship.

"I knew you would come," he said. "You always do."

"Yes," she answered, feeling sure that they had known each other quite well for a long time. "But this time I shall know what I am doing, and remember it afterwards."

"I wish I did," he said. "I never remember anything when I am awake. I don't know even that I know you."

"What do you call me — here?" she asked.

"Why — Adal, I think," he answered.

"And am I a boy or a girl?"

"A boy, of course — no, a girl — oh, really, I don't know!" He laughed in confusion. "But come on — the trumpets are sounding — we must ride against the infidel!"

By his side was a horse, saddled and ready, and she got up behind him. It seemed that they were both armoured and accoutred in the Templars' armour, and she had a long sword by her side. She remembered the device on the Templars' seal: two knights riding on one horse.

They galloped out of the orchard, and it was daylight. Before them lay a wide plain, and far off a little compact city on a hill, which she knew must be Jerusalem. Behind them she heard the squadron of the Templars riding, but she did not look back at them. Suddenly, as they rode toward the City, there rose up before them a host of ugly little swarthy men. On their heads were small red turbans with golden crescents. They all looked alike, with horrible grinning faces, and sharp crooked swords.

"Oh, what are these?" exclaimed Adela.

"Paynims, Saracens — have no fear of them — charge for the Cross!" He drew his sword and galloped into the thick of them. She drew her sword too, but passed it into her left hand so that as he slashed on the right she could slash on the left. In the body which she now seemed to have, her left arm was as good as her right.

They hewed at the swarthy little men, who fought fiercely and shouted, but fell as they slashed them, without any blood. They seemed to be made of something like soft wood, or wax, and did not bleed, nor did their expressionless faces show any pain. More and more came up on Hugh and Adela, who hewed them all down, rushing on through them with fierce delight. Behind them came the other Crusaders but never overtook them. At one moment Hugo drew rein, and Adela was able to look back. A few of the Crusaders had fallen, but over each one hovered a fine white-winged angel, just like those in the church paintings at home, gently drawing the man's soul out of his body, and carrying it upward.

The Holy City was nearer now, and shone with gold; on a pinnacle in the midst Our Lady stood, in a robe of blue, with the Holy Child in her arms. As the Crusaders fought their way toward the City through the tumbling little men, Our Lady smiled at Hugo and Adela and flung a handful of rose petals.

And then Adela was suddenly awake, and it was all a dream — or was it? The tips of her fingers smelt of roses.

There were galleries all round the great courtyard, and there Adela, her mother, and all the ladies of the company, were seated on chairs to watch a spectacle. Down below, the courtyard was thronged with armed men. With pomp and pageantry, a procession entered below. It was Count Raymond himself, with all his peers, glittering with metal and coloured silks, and a tall swordsman by his side, and men with a brazier. Adela supposed the brazier was to keep Count Raymond warm out there.

Then a long line of tall, dignified men were led in, in long white robes and turbans. Their arms were tied behind them. Their faces were pale, and their eyes dark, and all had beards, some black, some grey. They held themselves with sorrowful composure, as the foot soldiers led them along, and Adela was reminded of pictures she had seen of Christian martyrs.

"Oh, who are these?" she asked.

"Paynims, child — Saracens, Mussulmans, and heathens. These are the enemy."

"Oh —" But these were not in the least like the little men in the dream.

The first was led before Count Raymond in his chair. Now, Adela thought, he will loose his bonds and set him free. The paynim man made a low obeisance. Count Raymond gave a sign to the man with the sword. The sword fell, and the paynim's head toppled horribly to the ground. Indeed these were not like the little men who did not bleed . . . .

Another and another . . . there were some whose hands were chopped off . . . .

"They don't feel anything, those paynims," said Dame Blanche. "They'd serve our own men the same if they caught them. Anyway, they've refused baptism. Now this one will be a different punishment, look —"

"Let me go. I don't feel well," Adela said, shuddering, and escaped to her room, where she cried for hours.

It was some nights before she could get "through the Curtain" to Hugo again, but when she did, she told him about it, and all her horror and revulsion. He looked worried, and said, seriously, "How can we understand? All we know, when we are awake, is that we must obey and fight. But I know. I have felt it too."

But then the little swarthy men crept up on them, and once again they had to fight their way through them. This time they broke right through the Saracen army and came to the golden walls of the Holy City. And the gates stood open, and they went in. There was nobody to be seen there. All stood deserted, all the houses of gold, with their windows of jewels. But from somewhere, high up, a sound of heavenly music and joyful singing filled the air. From every part of the city could be seen the pinnacle where Our Lady stood.

"Come," said Hugo, "we must seek the Sepulchre of the Lord," and they went on through the golden streets, but somewhere the ways diverged, and Adela looked round for Hugo and he was not there. She went on, calling for him, and found herself outside the City on the other side, looking back at the walls.

And there before her, but facing the City, was the Saracen host — those same tall, turbaned, white-robed men, with pale faces and dark beards. They were armed and on horseback, and galloping, galloping toward the City. Out against them came a horde of little swarthy men, who looked exactly like those she had fought against with Hugo, just as ugly and as wooden, but with round red caps on their heads with silver crosses on them. And the Saracens charged into them, hewing and slicing off heads, arms and legs as before; and as before, the little men fell without bleeding and with no sign of pain. Before the Saracens, as they fought, stood the Holy City, but on the pinnacle where Adela had seen Our Lady, was a tall flowering tree. Some of the Saracens fell, and over each one hovered a beautiful girl, with butterfly wings and clothed in rainbow silks, who drew out his soul and carried it aloft.

Two Saracens closed up beside her.

"Come, lady," they said, "we welcome you with all honor." They led her away from the battle, to a richly decorated tent, where sat Saladin himself on silken cushions. He smiled and bade her welcome, and as she thought of the tall men slaughtered in the castle yard, her eyes filled with tears.

"Lady of the Giaours," he said, "if we all pitied our enemies, there would be no wars."

"And would not that be a good thing?" she said with the boldness of a dream.

"Ah, who knows? But we know that Allah made soldiers to fight. What else would they do?"

He made her sit on cushions by his side, and sip a strange sweet drink, and he gave her a password which she was to remember. Over and over he said it. And she woke up saying it. In the moment of waking she wrote it down, somehow, so that she should not forget it.

Everything was astir in the castle and town of Acre. "We shall have to move as soon as possible," said Sir Brian. "Get boats and be off tomorrow early. It isn't safe here. Saladin's forces are between us and

Tiberias. We're cut off. Tiberias is besieged, with Count Raymond's wife and family there. Some say the army is to march on Tiberias. Some say not. I know what *we'll* do. Get packed."

The rest of the day was full of bustle. But Adela, whose heart was heavy with foreboding, went to sleep early.

When she slipped out of her body, and went in search of Hugo, she knew there was a difference. She did not find herself in the moonlit orchard. She was not in the magical world of visions, but hovering over and wandering through the real world, like a ghost, unseen. She was watching the army of the Crusaders on the march, through the night, the Templars leading. Hugo was there, on his horse, but not riding gallantly. They were none of them riding gallantly. They laboured through the night on tired horses and drooped in their saddles. She heard them talking.

"Why on earth did we have to leave Sephoria? Plenty of water in Sephoria, and a good defensive position. But no — before we'd time even to water the horses —"

"And after marching all day — hardly time for a mouthful to drink, and God! I'm thirsty . . ."

"They say the commanders quarrelled. Count Raymond, like a sensible man, said stay in Sephoria, with the water, and wait a bit. Though, mind you, it's *his* wife and children who are in Tiberias. He said it was a trap to get us to move out. And King Godfrey listened to him, didn't he?"

"Yes, but then Count Gerard came in, and said Raymond was a traitor and had sold out to the Saracens. So King Godfrey got in a panic and ordered us to march on Tiberias at once, before we'd had any rest."

"What can you do, when your commanders disagree? Oh, what would I give for a drink! Never mind ale or wine. Just water."

"If we can get through to Galilee, there's plenty of water."

"And all the Saracens between us and Galilee. The horses will founder first."

"What's this place we're making for — the top of that hill?"

"They call it Hattin — the Horns of Hattin . . . the Horns of Hattin . . ."

She moved through the ranks and hovered over Hugo, trying to enter his mind. But all that came across to her was thirst, thirst, thirst — and the oppressive weight of his armour, the heat inside it, the weakness of the body that had sweated all day and was now drained dry. The grey-faced old Templars rode beside him, bidding him cheer up, for the more the suffering the greater the glory. He listened dull-eyed.

She woke, dry-throated, crying out, "Water, water — the Horns of Hattin, the Horns of Hattin . . ."

She knew what she had to do. Quietly she slipped out of bed and dressed in her riding breeches and corselet, but without the skirt, and threw a hooded mantle over her. Stealthily she slipped out to the horse-lines, found her own black mare, saddled her, and before she mounted, slung on her saddle two small casks full of water. It was as much as the mare could carry.

The sentry at the door barred her way.

"Oh!" she said. "Please . . ."

"Oh, a lady. By heaven, the Lady Adela!"

"Soldier," she said, "you know why people sometimes have reason to slip out alone?"

Certainly he did — with half the Castle engaged in love affairs.

"Surely — but *you*, Lady Adela. I'd never have thought *you* . . ."

In the dark he could not see her blush.

"All right, my lady. Not a word from me. But take care of yourself, won't you?" He let her pass.

Then she rode like the wind toward Tiberias.

From daybreak to noon she rode, and that noon was fiercely hot. It was July, and the grass was dry and the earth was splitting. Once in sheer exhaustion she dismounted, drank from a wayside spring and let the mare drink, and rested a short time. She could not have eaten if she had had food with her. Then she went on eastward, and as she went she could smell burning grass. Nothing unusual in that. The grass caught fire very easily at that season. But now the smoke grew dense. Soon it was a choking smother. As she came up a hill, and saw Galilee below her, she saw the battle too. It raged fiercely over the plateau — the Horns of Hattin! The army of the Cross, fighting fiercely, fighting desperately, against the vast, overwhelming army of the Saracens. As they fought, the smoke from the grass-fire, blowing away from the Saracens, covered the Crusaders in its stifling, throat-drying fog.

The foot-soldiers had broken away and fled. Most of the horses lay exhausted on the ground, and the knights were falling one by one, to lie, helpless heaps of metal, at their enemies' feet. This was no battle of little swarthy bloodless men. Far from it! Adela was spared nothing of the blood and horror.

Alone among the rest stood the Templars and the Hospitallers, grouped around the black-and-white banner, isolated in the field like the last sheaf to be reaped. They were laying about them fiercely, and Hugo was amongst them — but they were failing. As she watched she saw Hugo fall.

Without a moment's hesitation she spurred forward, forcing the unwilling mare to face the smoke. But there was rough cliff in front of her, and a drop — no way down. She had to go round, and the only way she could go led her in a curve to the opposite side of the battlefield. She found herself dashing into the lines of the Saracens. Hands reached up to catch her bridle-reins.

"Oh, let me go!" she exclaimed, not at all sure if they understood her language. "I must get to him. I must save a life — save life, do you understand?" The dark faces grinned, not comprehending. It seemed the battle was over. The Saracens were coming back from the field, leading prisoners.

Then Adela remembered the password she had learnt from Saladin in her dream, and spoke it.

The men fell back in astonishment, and let her through. Down that grim hillside she went, through the smoke. She tried to remember the place where she had seen Hugo fall by the black-and-white standard. The worst was having to pass the other men, wounded, dying, ghastly, who cried to her from the ground for water. Some of them were too parched to cry out. Some seemed to be unwounded. It was only the heat and the smoke and thirst that had killed them. But she could not spare any water. There were a few men who had enough strength to stagger to their feet and try to snatch the water-barrels. But she beat them off with her riding-whip. They had not much strength after all and could not run after her.

At last she found him.

He lay unmoving on a horrible heap of dead men. She dismounted, and dragged him aside to a clean patch of ground, where she bathed his face, trickled water into his mouth, and freed him from his armour. She had to use his dagger to cut its lacings; the metal was still hot to the touch. She flung each piece away from him. He began to stir, opened his eyes, and was able to swallow the water she held to his lips. She put a wet kerchief over his nostrils against the smoke. And when at last he showed enough signs of life, she helped him on to her mare, and mounted behind him, holding him, once again like two Templars on one horse, and so rode carefully away from that dreadful place. She went boldly through the camp of Saracens, using the password. The Saracens buzzed and chattered in amazement, and some of them sent messengers to tell Saladin, but they let Adela and Hugo through.

After a long time they halted by the sweet shores of Galilee, and she propped his back against a sycamore tree, and gave him water again. Then he took notice of her at last.

"Adal," he said. "My good comrade. I thought truly that we had been through Purgatory together, and were entering Paradise. But now I see that you are a woman."

"Are you glad or sorry?" she said.

"Oh, I'm glad, I'm glad!" he cried. "And yet — what am I saying? My vow — the Templars . . ."

Very gently she told him how the Templars and the Hospitallers lay on the battlefield. He crossed himself, and wept. Then he held out his arms to her as if she had been his mother.

"And now—but what shall we do, my love, what shall we do?"

"I know what we must do," she said. "We'll go to the Abbess of Shaston. She'll make everything right for us."

And the Abbess of Shaston did make everything right for them. She went all the way to Rome and persuaded the Pope to absolve the young Templar of his vows. So they were married and they named their first-born daughter Hodierna after the Abbess.

X.
THE
DEVIL
TO
PAY

The sisters of the Order of Saint Evodias and Saint Syntyche, on the crest of Shaston Hill, specialised in reconciling neighbours' quarrels, as Saint Paul urged Timothy to do for those two Roman ladies. They also sorted out the other troubles of the neighbourhood as best they could. Every day one or other of the nuns sat in the little sunny parlour looking into the garden, and listened to the complaints of any who came, and many opened griefs to them that they would not have told to a priest. All this was secret as the confessional, but everything was reported to the Abbess, who sat like a queen bee in her hive, considering, consulting, prescribing, compounding her own peculiar medicines, and often praying for those poor troubled folks.

The Abbess led a busy life. There were the Holy Offices to say in chapel, and the convent and its lands to run, besides her extensive and peculiar studies, but now and again she was not at her post. She was elsewhere. Let us watch her, on a certain winter evening.

She locked the door of her snug little room (her "cell"), and laid aside her canonical habit. She put on the coarse linen shift with loose sleeves tied in with coloured ribbons, the scarlet woolen gown, and the laced stays of a country bar maid. Over her dark brown hair — short, but not cropped — she tied a bright coloured scarf, and flung a skein of coloured beads round her neck: "tawdries" they were called, in honour of St Audrey and her Fair. She opened a very secret box, and took out a rose-coloured paste, which she applied a very little, to her cheeks and lips. (The box held other colours for other occasions.) Then, throwing a coarse woolen cloak around her, she stepped out discreetly by a back staircase, as convincing a tavern wench as you would never notice in a village street.

It was still daylight. She strode boldly through the little town, her limbs enjoying the freedom of her light clothing, the wind blowing the scarf over her hair. She passed one or two people known to her, but as they thought of the Abbess as a formal figure in white, with her face shadowed by wimple, gorget and veil, they of course did not really look at her.

There were several inns in Shaston; the largest, on the brow of the hill, being the "Cross in Hand," which had been greatly expanded to accommodate Crusaders who assembled there for the Journey to the Coast. But the Abbess made for one of the smaller ones — obscure and rather squalid. Quietly she slipped through a back door and hung her cloak in the kitchen. The cook and the two tavern maids greeted her as one of themselves and the landlord, "Wat the Lion," gave her a conspiratorial wink. He knew who she was, but the others did not.

"Come on, Audrey me maid, hurry up, we've a full house," he said. As she stepped out into the public room, the noise nearly knocked her down. It was a wide room, not very high, and lit with tallow candles in sconces, the smoke of which clouded the stale air. The place was packed shoulder-tight with men, shouting, laughing, drinking, singing, arguing and fighting — there were a couple of well-known whores, young and gaudy, their shrill voices rising above the roar of the men. The air was so foul that the weak tallow dips could scarcely burn. The two tavern maids were going through the crowd with trays of mugs, cups, glasses, and jugs. And soon the Abbess was doing the same. She served the drinks and busily collected the money, but all the time she was looking from face to face, seeking one in particular.

But she did not find it, and after five exhausting hours, she handed over the money to Wat, took off her apron and put on her cape, and slipped away to the convent. Too tired now to stride, she let herself in by her private postern, removed her disguise and became the Abbess again.

She did this for three nights running, and on the third night among the drovers and laborers, she found what she was looking for: a young man, who might have been handsome if he had not been so pale and haggard, dressed like a nobleman. His clothes were rich in colour and fine in fabric, well-cut, but neglected, crumpled, and dirty. His black hair fell in damp streaks over his forehead, and his eyes burned as if with fever. The Abbess, shuddering, felt that she was looking at the face of damnation. He was drinking recklessly, laughing loudly, and talking nonsense. Sometimes he grew quarrelsome, raised his voice, swore, and then, slumping down in a sulk at a table with his head on his hands, called for more wine, drank and grew lively again.

The Abbess was very tired, but she could not leave; she had to watch the young nobleman. The other patrons of the inn began to depart in twos and threes and noisy parties. The other two girls put on their cloaks and went home. Wat tidied up, locked away the money and went upstairs. As he passed the Abbess he said quietly, "I'm up there if you want me." But she replied, "Thanks, no need, but just tell me, is that Lord Romuald of Linhead?"

"Yes, that's Lord Romuald, God help him."

Everyone had gone now. Lord Romuald sat with his head resting on his arms on the table. He seemed asleep or unconscious. The Abbess stood back in the shadows, waiting until the last footsteps had died away and old Wat had stopped moving overhead.

The fire in the great hearth under the chimney flickered and died down. The tallow candles went out one by one and the room was dark. Then a shaft of moonlight pierced the darkness.

The Abbess stepped quietly forward and laid a hand on the sleeping man's shoulder. He snorted, opened his eyes painfully and groaned. He pushed back his chair noisily and staggered outside. She heard him vomiting. Presently he came back, groping like a sleepwalker, and dropped back into the same chair, still with his arms resting limply on the table. By this time she had lit a candle.

He began talking as if to himself . . .

"Oh God . . . oh God . . . oh God . . . Now why do I say 'God' when I can't pray? Oh God, let me die . . . oh no, God, don't let me die. I can't face it — I daren't die, and I can't bear to live. What am I to do?"

She came closer to him and faced him across the table.

"My lord," she said quietly, "what is your sorrow?"

"What is my sorrow? One asks, what is my sorrow?" Suddenly he seemed to notice her. "Who are you?"

"Why, I'm just Audrey, the tavern wench."

"Audrey, oh then, Audrey, come here and comfort me a little."

His brow was beaded with sweat; his lips were quite bloodless. She could see his hands were shaking. She went round the table and came close to him, and he put out his arms and gathered her to him like a lonely and frightened child with a comforting doll. She let him caress her — thus far and no further. But she could feel there was little lust in his touch, only fear and pain, and terrible need of reassurance. She soothed him like a child, drawing his head down upon her breast. Her pity for him transcended every other thought.

"Tell me," she murmured.

"Oh, Audrey, dear girl, oh, how can I?"

"Go on. Tell me."

"No sleep, except when I'm drunk, and then my dreams are horrible. I'm afraid to sleep, and I'm so tired. I wish I could die, but I'm afraid . . . afraid . . . afraid. Once I was afraid of nothing, and look at me now. I'd end it all, but if I die, I'll go to *him*."

"To *him*? Who is he?"

"Haven't you guessed?"

"Not the . . . the Evil One?"

"Yes."

He hid his face again on her bosom and she could feel tears trickling down between her breasts, and the shudders that shook him. A deep horrified silence fell between them. It was so quiet she could hear a mouse rustling in the panelling. Then he lifted his head again.

"He owns me, body and soul. I sold myself to him. Look, here is the pact I signed — I carry it about with me though I hate it, because I dare not let it be found." He drew back a little, sought for something in the pocket of his doublet, and drew it out. It was a much-folded piece of parchment, scribbled, blotched, and charred at the edges.

"Signed with my blood, and sealed with fire."

She took it from him and looked at it curiously in the dim light.

"And have you received what he promised to give you?"

"Oh no." He had moved away from her and was standing up and staring into the fire.

"Why then, the agreement is void. What did you agree with him for?"

"Alicia," he said with a profound sigh. "My wife. He was to bring her back to me, alive in her body. He said he would."

"He is a deceiver, my lord. That is a thing he cannot do."

"He promised me, but now he says I must do more for him before he will give her to me. Listen, I'll tell you. She, my wife — and I loved her so — she died of a stillborn child, and that was my crime. I put that doom upon her. For four days I bore up and endured my sorrow, until they took her from the house and I saw them bury her. Then I came back to the empty house, and I could not bear it. I could not bear it. And then a tall dark man came in — I had not heard him come in — and stood over me and said, 'What would you give to have her back again, in human flesh and blood?' And I said, 'My heart, my soul, my body, my whole self, all that I am.' And he said, 'Agreed. so shall it be. Only sign this parchment.' And . . . and I signed, he pressed his thumb on the parchment to seal it, and it burned at his touch. And so it was done."

She looked into his bone-white face as he stared into the fire, and if it had seemed to her before as the face of damnation, now it was far, far worse.

"Why did you not go to a priest?"

"I couldn't. I couldn't, and besides, what could a priest do? I am damned by my own hand. A priest would turn from me in horror and bid me go where I belong."

She held the parchment and presently slipped it into the pocket of her gown. He put his arms round her again, and went on talking miserably, pitifully.

"And still he does not give her to me. He says I must do more for him. He wants blood, blood. I have given him blood. I tried small animals — a poor little cat. The poor, poor little thing, a stray dog, a deer, a horse, oh, God forgive me, one of the horses out of my own stable — there was blood enough there." The shuddering fit shook him again. "But *he* says it is not enough. He will have the blood of a child."

Now the Abbess was trembling, almost as much as he was.

"But you need not do these fearful things," she said. "Why do you obey him?"

"I am in his power now. He will not let me go. I must obey his horrible hests."

He fell back in the chair and laid his head on the table.

"Get me something to drink, for the Lord's sake. I'm parched."

She went across the room and filled a goblet with dry red wine, adding a little water. She also added something she carried in her hand. When she brought it to him, he caught her in his arms again.

"Marie . . . Dorothy . . . no, Audrey. You're a kind wench, and you haven't run away in horror from a poor wretch like me." A little colour came back into his face. "Take me up to your bedchamber, Audrey."

"I've no bedchamber here, my lord."

"Then any quiet corner."

She put his hands gently away from her. She had foreseen this, but the drug would work very soon now. There was something, however, that she must know.

"Presently, my lord. But tell me, this frightful offering you have to make, when is it to be?"

"When the moon is next eclipsed."

"And do you know when that will be?"

"No, but I guess it must be at the time when the moon is next full. I have to watch the skies."

"And where?"

His head was drooping forward on the table again.

"At the Mare and Nine . . ."

He toppled sideways from the chair, unconscious. She put a cushion under his head before she slipped quietly home.

The Mare and Nine Foals, she knew it. One of those grim, forsaken stone circles, away on the downs toward the sea. Nine standing stones there were, and three larger stones grouped together with one other on top of them. That was the Mare, no doubt the Nightmare, and around her were her nine grim children. Men shunned that place.

The Abbess had, among other unusual accomplishments, the ability to predict eclipses, by certain curious mathematical arts, chiefly founded upon the number of stones at Stonehenge, such as might well have brought her under suspicion of witchcraft as well as heresy, were it not for her influential connections. She was, therefore, after a great deal of intricate ciphering, able to predict an eclipse of the moon in three weeks' time. She prepared herself in various ways.

The night of the predicted eclipse was still and windless, but with a certain haziness on the horizon, a certain tension in the air. The Abbess sat watching by her window. She watched the full moon rise, and after what seemed a long time, a little shadow, not more than a thread, creep upon the round white disc and thicken slowly.

She stood up, and took her white mantle which lay ready beside her. Suddenly from the courtyard below came a scream of anguish, a scream that went on and on . . . .

There was a hasty knock at the door. Sister Ruth was there shaking. She was usually very calm.

"Oh, Reverend Mother, the wife of Geoffrey the cowman, she says Lord Romuald — the mad lord — burst in on them within this half hour, snatched up her baby from its cradle without a word, flung down a bag of gold on the floor, and was gone, riding his black horse."

The Abbess gave a deep gasp, not of dismay but rather as of a swimmer meeting the expected icy water. She raised a silencing hand to Sister Ruth.

"As I foresaw. Very well, with God's help I'm ready. Tell the poor woman all may yet be well. Let her pray for me, and you, sisters, pray for me, all of you, with all your might."

She put on her white mantle but took off her wimple and gorget, covering her head with a white scarf. For if he sees me wimpled and veiled, she reasoned, he will not know me and he will not trust me.

The Mare and Nine Foals was an eerie place even by daylight, and terrible in fair moonlight, but now the light of the moon was failing, degree by degree as that dark-red disc spread slowly over its face and all the sky grew livid. Lord Romuald on his black horse came echoing up the stony path. His left hand held the reins, but his right arm clutched a bundle under his cloak. The child was asleep. The soft warm body rested against his side, and as he thought what he had to do, a terrible sick spasm shook him, and cold chills ran over his body.

He dismounted, carefully holding the child, and tethered the horse to a crouching thornbush. Past a high turf bank crowned with bushes he walked through an opening, and there was the circle before him, a space of grass pale in the ghastly light, marked all round with the towering monoliths, and at the farthest end the great trilithon, The Mare, the mother of all nightmares. Under her shadow a small fire was burning.

He could see no one, hear nothing, yet he felt that someone was there, someone he did not want to see. He moved resolutely toward the fire. Somewhere a dog began to howl, a thin eerie sound. He was reminded of the poor dog he had slain; it had howled so when he had led it to this place. And now the baby on his arm woke and began to cry.

Between him and the fire a wide circle had been marked out on the turf with small white stones. He approached it and cast a glance up toward the moon. The shadow was more than half over the white face now. Only a crescent of red light remained, outlining the moon on the wrong side. His eyes were drawn back to the stones. Something stood there, silently, all in black with its face hidden. Romuald could feel the evil power reaching out from that figure.

It spoke, in a hollow voice.

"Draw near."

Where Romuald stood, a tree cast its shadow. The grass beneath it was dappled with little crescents of light, like the sick moon above.

Romuald started to move forward across the grass circle, toward the fire and the figure that stood there. He felt a strong compulsion to see the eyes under the cowl. Straining, he seemed to see them, and they compelled him step by step. Behind him now he heard the thumping of hoofs.

He could not guess what the sound brought — another fiend? A human enemy? Perhaps the justice of man about to descend upon him, strike him down for the dreadful thing he was about to do. He would almost have welcomed it, a sword or a halter . . . .

"Come," said the black presence. The last vestige of the moon was gone. Only a dull red nimbus glowed round a circle of blackness, against a strange slatey sky; all nature was in unnatural darkness, full of ghostly livid colours. The ill-omened darkness, like a spell, silenced everything. Except the hoofs.

The child struggled in his arms, and broke the silence with its cries. He shook it, pressed it, clumsily, feeling all the panic of a man unused to babies. It wriggled in his arms, arching its back, its clothing was wet and sickening, its wide-open mouth seemed to take up all its face, as it screamed and screamed. His impulse was to drop it, or to put a hand over that squalling gap and stop its breath with the noise — but no, he had to present it alive, and then . . . .

A few more steps brought him before the fire and the great overarching stones. The cowled figure said:

"Now."

Holding the child, as best he could, supine over his left arm, Romuald drew his dagger. He could hear the hoofbeats stop, and human steps coming toward him. Then a voice broke in clearly.

"Hold! You will not do this thing."

A white form came walking quickly into the ring of standing stones, glimmering against the dark hedge even in that dim light. A woman in a long white mantle, her hair unveiled save for a floating scarf, she came through the circle of white pebbles as if she did not fear it. She held out her arms for the baby, and Romuald gladly let her take it. She gathered it up into her white mantle and turned to face the hooded black figure. It spoke, in a deep hissing tone of malice.

"Give up that child."

"Give up this man!" she replied.

"Not for you, miserable daughter of man."

To the Abbess, the black figure seemed gigantic.

"You puny mortal," it was saying, "get out from under my feet, or I will crush you."

She seemed to see its feet under the long cloak. They were like a bear's feet, long, bony and hairy with clutching sharp claws. She felt herself to be a tiny particle between those ugly toes, so tiny they could not find her.

"Fiend," she said, "I am too small for you to crush. I am down in the dust under your feet, but I can sting you, and I will. Not in my own strength, but in my Master's."

"Your master cannot prevail against me."

"You lie! As always, you lie! Listen, and I will speak the name of my Master, at which every knee shall bow, of things in heaven, and things on the earth, and things under the earth. For you also believe and tremble. In the name of Jesus Christ, Son of the Living God, I charge you, demon, release this man, whom you have enslaved, and depart from hence to the place prepared for you."

As she spoke, the moon showed the first faint shimmer of returning light.

The cowled figure seemed to shrink and shake. Yet it stood its ground.

"I hear, but I will not release this man yet. Let your God of Justice give me my due. There is a quittance to pay. If I leave this man's soul . . . "

"And body," put in the Abbess.

"I say nothing of his body, but if I release his soul, I will have that infant as the price."

"By the Splendour of the Most High!" cried the Abbess, and her voice soared to the sky, where the moonlight was growing minute by minute. "That you shall not! The child is not his, nor yours, nor mine, but God's." She clasped the child close to her — it had stopped crying from the moment she had taken it and was now quietly asleep. "Liar and father of lies, this man owes you nothing."

With her free hand she sought and found the parchment Romuald had given her.

"Look, deceptive fiend," she said. "Here is his indenture. In return for his soul and body, you promise to restore to him his wife Alicia in human flesh and blood, to live with him until he too dies, when this bill shall fall due for full payment. There you have promised something you cannot perform. Only God could give her back to him. All you could give, after forcing him into the shedding of more and more innocent blood, would be a simulacrum, a mere empty shell, ensouled perhaps by a demon, a vain thin mask, that would fail and fall to pieces as soon as it was touched. Look, you cheating merchant, you have promised a thing you cannot perform. Look well, do you see it? Then this pact is no pact at all, this bond is worth less than the parchment it is written on. Thus!"

She tore the tough parchment across, hard and resistant as it was, and flung both halves, with all its seals and strings, into the fire. The dry oily substance rolled up, shrivelled, smoked, burst into flames and was consumed. She watched till the last fragment fell into black dust. Romuald watched with her. As for the creature in black, it stood rigid, and Romuald heard it give one deep sigh — then there seemed no more breath within the black cloak.

"Do you linger here still, fiend?" said the Abbess. "What are you waiting for? Give up your fragile borrowed shape, and depart unto the place prepared for you."

Her long white arm, two fingers outstretched, pointed at the dark shape. Above, the moon had become a waxy crescent.

The long black mantle fell, and the body within it stood naked. The body of an old man, aged but not reverend, his wrinkled greyish flesh drooping, palsied, his ragged white locks falling from his bald pate, his drooling beard straggling below his toothless mouth. For a moment he stood there, hideous but impotent, then, like the burnt parchment, the shape crumbled, shrivelled and was gone. The Abbess stepped to the spot where the fiend had stood, and stamped four times on the dust.

"Come away from this place," she said to Romuald. The mild moonlight filled the sky. They rode together, he on his black horse, she on her white one, with the baby clasped in the crook of her arm.

He turned and looked at her. "Who are you?" he said. "And where have I seen you before?"

"Never mind that now," she said, unsmiling. She was very tired.

As they came to the long slope which led toward Shaston, she said, "Go on without me, and wait for me at the door of the convent chapel."

"The convent chapel?"

"Yes, you have nothing to be afraid of now."

Geoffrey the cowman and his wife had sat all night by their small fire, weeping and praying over the empty cradle. The hut had no windows, but through cracks and crevices they had seen the moonlight darken above them, and shuddered; but the moonlight had cleared again, and now the daylight grew, but they still sat in misery.

Then the rough door was opened, and a woman stood there, a tall and beautiful woman in white, her head covered with a floating veil, and a baby in her arms.

They scrambled to their feet, and then dropped again to their knees.

"Oh, . . . oh . . . Holy Mary, Mother of . . ."

The woman spoke in a sweet voice but severely.

"Don't say it. Give God the glory. I'm nothing of the kind. Here, mother, take your son again, he's sound and well, and no harm has come to him, body or soul. Keep the bag of gold for his guerdon — there's no curse on it now."

"Oh, blessed lady, blessed Saint whoever you are . . ."

"I tell you, I'm no saint! Or if you must call upon a saint, light your candles to Saint Audrey, for I have heard she was but an indifferent saint."

Before she reached the door of the convent chapel, the Abbess had wrapped the white scarf closely round her face and neck. Romuald was waiting for her.

"But you, you are the . . ."

She laid her finger on her lips.

"Not a word. Now go in, yes, go into the chapel. Do not be afraid of anything you may see there."

He went in, and she came close behind him.

By the altar, within the communion rail, a woman was standing, young and golden-haired, in a sky-blue robe touched with gold.

Romuald started forward with a cry, and then drew back, still afraid.

"All is well," said the Abbess's voice behind him. "This is your Alicia, in truth, yes, the Most High has permitted her to come to you just for one moment – *'quia multum amavit'* – because you loved deeply."

The golden-haired woman came through the communion rails, and embraced Romuald. Her touch was warm, and her body was solid and comforting.

"Just for one moment, Romuald," she said. "Just to tell you I am still with you. Do not weep any more. Take up your life. I shall be near you in the Holy

Mass. And I will send you a messenger, my dear, who will love you and bear your children. Receive her for my sake."

She kissed him, and then stood back from him with her arms outstretched. One smile, and she was suddenly gone. Romuald sank on his knees and gave way to healing tears.

XI.
THE
WYF-WOLF ⸺⸺⸺⸺⸺⸺⸺⸺

Winter lay like a grey winding-sheet over all of England, and not least over the great forest, part of which the Romans called Anderida, that stretched from the east coast to the midlands. Man and beast alike were pinched with hunger. But in the convent of Shaston (called the convent of Evodias and Syntyche), faces were less pale and hearts less heavy than in most houses. For though the nuns there kept Lent in due fashion, the Abbess had the cunning devices she had brought from the Holy Land, and a store of foreign spices, syrups, and conserved fruits. Not only were there winter pippins and dried plums on their table, but dates and figs, citrons and lemons, for the sisters, the lay-sisters, and even the servitors, with plenty left to go to the daily beggars and the poorest cottagers. With that and the proper allowance of good ale and wine, Lent was bearable. The little school that the sisters kept for the neighbours' children had to close, for the journey up or down the ice-bound slope, where Shaston stands, was too hard for the children. But almost every day the Abbess rode out on her tall horse with her faithful attendant Bil and visited the scattered houses in the woods, with gifts of her own concocting and with her elixirs and electuaries to cure their ailments.

But this morning, there was trouble. She looked up from her writing.

"Well, well! So it's Sister Huldah. Why have you brought her here, guarded like a prisoner? What has the poor thing done?"

Sister Huldah, a tall, bony woman, yellow of face and wild of eye, stood between friendly Sister Ruth and stolid Sister Deborah. The latter spoke.

"Reverend Mother, she disobeys your rule."

The Abbess focussed her large blue eyes on the culprit.

"How's this, Sister Huldah?"

She had watched Sister Huldah carefully, ever since that poor nun had been sent to her by the neighbouring Benedictine convent at Wareham. The Abbess of Wareham had sent her out of fear for her life because of her excessive austerities. It was thought that perhaps the milder rule of Saints Evodias and Syntyche might persuade the poor thing to give her body a chance to recover.

Sister Huldah lowered her head in silence.

"She refuses to eat the fruit and sweetmeats your Ladyship gives us," said Sister Deborah.

"Why, Sister Huldah? Don't you like them?"

Sister Huldah looked up at those searching eyes.

"Oh yes, Reverend Mother," she said, "but they are not for me. I cannot eat them."

"But my dear child, don't you understand? These things are not given you simply for pleasure, but so that you and all the others may keep well till winter ends, and have the strength to do each one her duties. If they find them pleasant, so much the better. What say you?"

"Oh, my lady, Reverend Mother, they are too pleasant for me. I cannot partake of any pleasure."

"But why, in God's truth, can you not?" The Abbess was becoming impatient.

"Because I am a miserable sinner, and the chief of sinners."

"We are all sinners, child. You must go to shrift and confess your sin, and be absolved."

"Oh no, Reverend Mother, I cannot. No priest would absolve me."

"Daughter, it is possible to sin through pride at the greatness of a sin."

Something like a sob wrenched the poor creature's bony bosom.

"Sin upon sin! Oh no, perpetual penance for me. Your syrups and sweets — no, no. Bread and water and dried fish are all I must eat — for the rest of my life."

"But, dear saints above!" exclaimed the Abbess. "You will be costive."

"I am costive. Does it matter?"

Patiently as to a child, the Abbess explained to her why it mattered. As she talked, she could tell that the poor culprit was relaxing a little. The Abbess

leaned forward and covered Sister Huldah's cold
hand with her warm one. Before she dismissed her,
she had persuaded her to eat two dates and a morsel
of ginger, and to drink a cup of hot mint-water. She
sent her away, not as under escort, but under Sister
Ruth's special care, with instruction to mind her
tenderly, and see that she took a daily matin-draught
of fish-oil, which Huldah could hardly refuse, because it was very nasty.

The Abbess thought long about Sister Huldah.
Poor thing, mortifying herself unnecessarily. After
all, Sister Huldah was the best teacher in their little
school, very kind and loving to all the children. No
doubt she missed the children who could not come
because of the snow. When the thaw came (oh,
please God, soon!) the classes would recommence,
and perhaps the poor sister would be happier.

But the day was short, and the Abbess must go on
her rounds of friendly visits before early dusk. She
rang for Bil and ordered her horse to be made ready,
wrapped herself warmly and was off into the woods,
Bil sometimes bringing his horse up near to chat
with her, for Bil was an old and trusted friend.

The forest, even on its outskirts, was strange and
unfriendly. In the summer she knew and loved it
well. It was "the merry greenwood," but now, deep
under snow, it was sinister. The snow had stopped
falling; now and then the heavy masses of it that
sagged all the branches fell with a whispering sound,

as a tree released its burden. There seemed to be no birds nor beasts nor any kind of life.

"How quiet it is, Bil," she said. "Too quiet. I don't like it. Did you hear the wolves last night?"

"Yes, my lady," he said. (He always addressed her as "my lady," being a Saxon, not as "Madame," as the adherents of the French families would do.) "Indeed, they were howling and hunting."

"Hunting? What would they find to hunt? Bil, do you believe that the wolves are creatures of the Devil, not of the Good Lord at all?"

"Why no, my lady. They're God's creatures like the rest of us. You see, my lady, when there was nothing but wolves, before our long-fathers came here, the wolves lived on the deer, and the deer bred in numbers, and there was enough for all. But since the folk came in and cleared the acres to make the farms, there's less room for the deer, and so less deer for the wolves. And so the wolves must do as best they can and take what the Good Lord sends them, though sometimes it's cattle, or sheep in the lambing, or . . ."

He broke off as that long, blood-chilling howl came down to them faintly, from far away.

At that moment they both noticed the tracks, the first they had seen, of beasts and birds of many kinds, going down the path they themselves were taking. The Abbess had chosen the road to the glen where the mill stood by the river. The miller's family were friends of hers, the three little girls in particular who were always regular in their attendance at the school. She was anxious that they should receive their share of food and medicine.

As they followed the descending path, the tracks became more dense; as they came out into the open, they saw why. A complete ring had been formed, of all sorts of birds and beasts, but all of the flesh-eating kind, around something in the centre. There were foxes and weasels and stoats, martens and polecats; there were crows and kites and kestrels, rats and even a snake, all gathered into a silent ring, as if they wished to approach the thing in the centre, but dared not come closer to it, all hungrily longing for the fresh meat. The thing in the centre was a young deer, certainly slain that day.

The Abbess and Bil reined up their horses and halted outside the strange ring. The creatures, even the shyest of them, took no notice of their approach. Only the birds fluttered and changed their places from time to time. Among them the Abbess recognized one, larger than the rest: a raven. He was a frequent visitor to the convent back door. She used to feed him specially and was trying to teach him to talk as some men taught magpies. She called him Hector, and he could pronounce it, though his range of sounds was very limited.

The Abbess stretched out a hand to him, and called, "Hector!"

He hopped toward her and stood looking at her first with one eye and then with the other.

"Hector," he repeated.

She noticed how poorly he was looking. His black back-feathers had no gloss, his wings were straggling and ragged, his noble blue-black colour was dusty, his tail drooped, the points of his wings dragged along the ground.

"Why, Hector," she exclaimed, and offered him her gloved arm to perch upon like a hawk. "What is it, Hector boy?"

The bird turned its head to fix her with one eye.

"Horror," it said. "Horror, horror, horror."

She brought her head down toward him. "What horror, Hector? Tell me."

In reply he made a sound like "oo-geroo . . . oo-geroo . . ."

Just a foolish noise, one might have said, but to the Abbess it made sense, and very terrifying sense too.

"Is it *loup-garou?*"

He dipped toward her, and repeated, "oo-geroo . . . oo-geroo . . ."

The Abbess uttered a gasp. "Bil, do you hear that? The *loup-garou* — the werewolf."

"Oh God," he exclaimed, and crossed himself. The Abbess crossed herself too.

"All right, Hector," she said. "Go along now. Go to the back door of the convent, and the sisters will give you something." But her voice shook.

Bil dismounted and stepping carefully over the circle of spellbound creatures, looked carefully at the slain deer.

"Yes," he said as he rejoined the Abbess, "it's the work of a werewolf, sure enough. The carcass was drained of blood. See, that's why the creatures are behaving that way. They want the meat, they're starving, but they daren't come near it, for they smell the werewolf. Come, my lady, I think you'd better go home."

"No," she said. "I must go down to the mill. I fear the worst."

The mill was down in a wooded glen by the side of the stream. Usually the approach to the mill was crowded and lively, full of men and animals and wagons, with all the business of loading and offloading corn and flour, with shouts and curses and laughter, but not now.

No men, no wagons, nothing but a few chickens strutting aimlessly up and down, and there was a profound fearful silence. There were garments and such, scattered about. At the entrance to the further woods, what seemed like a bundle of clothes cast away . . . .

"No, don't look, my lady," said Bil. "It will make you sick."

"Nonsense, Bil. I've seen worse in the Holy Land." But when she came over and looked, she lost some of her assurance.

"Oh, poor little Ellen . . . ."

They rode home in silence.

"Bil," she said presently, "you'll go back with a couple of men — soon, before it's dark — and fetch the poor child in for burial."

"Yes, my lady, at once. But, my lady, who can it be?"

She thought it over, with shuddering. The werewolf never knew what he had become, people said. By daylight he went among his fellows, and at night, and especially when the moon was full, he changed. He might be anyone, the serving-men, the lay-brothers at the monastery of Saint Peter's, the man who brought in hay for the animals — he was half-witted, and some people were afraid of him — any of the folk in the town — even, God forbid, her faithful Bil himself.

Came the evening office, and even with the candles and the smell of incense and the reassuring words of the office, she was in fear and doubt.

"Sisters," she said, "let us pray for the soul of little Ellen at the mill, who has been torn apart by wild beasts."

There was a smothered sound from the back benches. Sister Huldah had risen, and with her veil pressed to her face stumbled blindly out. The infirmarian, who sat next to the chapel door, followed her quickly.

"Yes, poor Sister Huldah," the infirmarian reported later to the Abbess. "I found her vomiting her heart out at the end of the cloister. She had been very much attached to the little Ellen."

"Poor creature, poor creature," said the Abbess.

"I've sent her to bed. There was little else I could do," said the infirmarian.

Lying sleepless in her bed, the Abbess considered what to do. She decided that as a first step she must try to enter the werewolf's mind and find out who he was. So, in the light of the great cold full moon, she went through certain mental processes, and spoke certain words. But she must have used too powerful a spell.

Waking with a start, she was impelled to leap from her bed, and all in one movement, out through the window. She noticed her hands first, and her arms — they were covered with grey hair. Looking down at herself, she perceived how her body had changed. She was now a four-footed beast, muscular and springy. She felt no burden of clothing upon her and leapt and ran, enjoying her freedom. She had undoubtedly "shape-changed" herself into a wolf, but her mind and thoughts remained human. She knew that at any moment she could recall the words and actions that would change her back. She had not meant to become wholly an animal, but having gone so far, she would go on and find who the werewolf was.

Through the moonlit snowscape she let her feet carry her to the place where the wolves were. A remote dell, under the scooped-out roots of old trees, was their gathering place. She found them, dim recumbent shapes of grey fur, nose on paws, waiting for their leader's signal. They took no notice of her as she slipped in amongst them. There were seven of them beside herself. Four young males, the leader, who was a huge old male, and one female. The female drew up close beside her. Something like speech passed between them, a soft rumbling sound, which her mind somehow changed into words:

"I'm glad you've come. I had hoped you would."

The transformed Abbess looked closely at her. Yes, there was a kind of red light running up and down the wolf's body that was not on any of the others. The Abbess could guess by the long, leathery teats that this one was nursing young. Again she looked — and the animal had the tortured eyes of Sister Huldah.

She had not expected that the werewolf would prove to be a female — not a "were-wolf" but surely "wyf-wolf."

The female wolf turned to her. "Come, we'll run together," she seemed to say, for the head of the pack was bestirring himself. He drew himself up, stiff-legged, cast back his head, and emitted that long, high, terrifying howl. In the Abbess's mind it conveyed the words: "Come . . . deer . . . hunt . . . blood . . . meat . . ."

Instantly the pack followed him, the two females together. The exhilaration of running caught hold of the Abbess. She exulted in her freedom, in the sharp ice-cold air, in the smells and distant scents of the night, in the fellowship of running bodies — faster, faster — a great cry gathered itself in her lungs, and as those in front brought down the quarry, she flung herself with a howl upon the palpitating animal, and like the rest of them, buried her teeth in the soft raw flesh, avidly drinking the warm blood, which seemed to give her new life, which she needed desperately. Somewhere in her mind, a long way off, her human self was protesting: "This is horrible, this is dreadful. Oh, God forgive me!" But it was very far away, and the food was near . . . .

There was little enough flesh on this starved doe. The wolves began to fight for the food amongst themselves. The leader growled, shook some of them by the neck, called them together again. The wyf-wolf drew the Abbess aside.

"Come," she was saying, again without words, "no good here. Not enough blood — too many to share it. I know a better prey. Come with me."

She led the Abbess away in the opposite direction from the pack. She seemed to be saying: "Come, I'll show you no tough old goats, but young ones, young, tender, lovely. I fed there last night, down by the mill. Nobody there now, they all ran to the woodcutter's in the next valley. One small one I had, but there're two more. Come quick!"

The Abbess's rational mind, far away, came to her again. She tried to turn the she-wolf, whose side pressed against her as she ran. She could say nothing — say? Why, there was no saying here — but thinking hard she pressed against her companion, who continued her wordless speech.

"This way, not that way. Up through the oaks, where the path is. I must have blood, I must have blood, to give me milk for my little ones. Yes, my little ones, my two little wolf-cubs left in the den, Romulus and Remus."

The Abbess almost laughed in the midst of her horror, at the incongruity of the two old legendary names. But she exerted all her strength to turn the wyf-wolf from her purpose. The woodcutter's hut . . . and there were the distraught parents, and the two surviving little sisters. . . .

"Oh, you're pushing me the wrong way. Leave me, you stupid bitch."

They were getting nearer and nearer the woodcutter's hut. The Abbess thrust hard, jumping at last in front of the wyf-wolf. With a wild snarl, the wyf-wolf bared her fangs and sank them into her companion's throat. The Abbess's strength was spent, and she went down under the other's fierce onset, and felt those fangs in her neck. She shook them off as she fell, but the other came back and thrust toward her throat. With a desperate effort, the Abbess recovered the words that were the means of restoration. Everything swirled round her, and the great full moon seemed to float right over her; then she perceived she was in her own shape and in her own bed, and Sister Huldah lay on top of her, trying to reach her throat with those big white teeth. Instinctively the Abbess put her arm across her neck, opposing the point of her elbow against the attacker.

Now Sister Huldah was speaking in words.

"Give me blood. You must give me blood. It's for my children, my two little boys."

The Abbess knew all she needed to know about women who were seized with lust for their own sex, but this was different. This was no lust, but something worse and stranger.

The only light in the cell was the light of that baleful moon, but in that glow she saw that Sister Huldah had reached out to seize the little table-dagger which had been carelessly left on the small bed-side table.

Sister Huldah went on muttering as she struggled.

"My two little children! I bore them all alone in the woods, hiding my shame. I left them there, nobody knew. What else could I do? Give me blood, give me blood. Months after, I came back to the place. There were their little white bones, that was all. But now they cry to me, day and night, to feed them. I have no milk. You must give me blood, so that I can give them milk. Keep still, you silly she-wolf, and let me get at your throat!"

In horror and terror almost beyond prayer, the Abbess fought with the madwoman. Then the struggle changed direction.

"You'll not let me. Only one way, then, to get enough blood for my poor babes" — and the distraught woman jabbed the little knife in beneath her own ribs.

A deep sob and a gush of blood, then the Abbess, still halfway out of her body, saw the soul of Huldah drag itself free — her own soul followed it, and they were out together over the convent roofs. Then the soul of Huldah tried to plunge downward, but the Abbess kept hold of her and pushed upward. Upward and downward the two souls strove in the sky. The Abbess could not hear the stir in the convent as the nuns broke in upon the scene, but all her instinct was to struggle upward, and resist the other who tried to sink into some frightful and unimaginable depth below. The Abbess could not consciously pray, but all her impulse and the direction of her being was like a prayer, and suddenly she was above the moon, and someone caught hold of her adversary, saying quietly, "She is safe with us. You must go back."

When the nuns broke in upon them, and found them lying in a pool of blood, at first they thought both women were dead. The Abbess said nothing, especially about the small knife that was found in the bed. But she insisted that Sister Huldah be given

Christian burial, and the Absolution of Sins be pronounced over her. "She has suffered enough," she said.

XII.
SEEKING
WHOM
HE
MAY
DEVOUR ─────────────────

There was a stir in the courtyard. The Abbess Jovetta came bustling through, and was met by her guest the Abbess Hodierna.

"I don't know what to do, Hodierna," she said, using the familiar form of address because nobody else was present. "There's a band of strange men, very black and bearded — priests they seem to be, but I can't understand their language, and they don't speak Latin. They have a sort of box with them, and as far as I can understand, they want to give it to us."

"Let me see them," said the Abbess of Shaston. "You're sure they're not Greeks, or Jews? Well, then . . . ."

The strangers, some five or six, stood huddled together in the middle of the courtyard, like frightened cattle. In their midst was the box, a thing about three feet by two by two, made of wood overlaid with dark metal, perhaps bronze. It was wrought all over with figures, images of some fantastic kind. Not like the usual religious images, nor yet the well known pagan sort, Greek or Roman, that men sometimes unearthed. The Abbess's eyes were constantly drawn to those images, and her mind was led off by them from minute to minute into a dead reverie. She resisted the spell and came back to the men before her. She spoke various languages to them, but the priests, black-bearded and almost black-faced, trembled and showed the whites of their eyes, alarmed at the sounds of the words. At last they responded to one language. It was Coptic. Unfortunately, she knew little Coptic, and the flood of words she now released from them was intelligible to her only in fragments.

From what she could gather, they were the priests of the old Coptic Church; for centuries they had occupied a corner of the roof of the Church of the Holy Sepulchre. Now, frightened by something, they were leaving. They were going "over there —" a vague wave of the hand — because the Saracens were coming. Oh yes, the Saracens were coming — if not this year, then next year — oh, but perhaps tomorrow, only God knew — but they had a sign. What sign? Oh, that was too difficult. But they were in flight. And they wanted to leave the box behind for safe keeping, though they would not say what was in it.

"Is it a saint's relic?" she asked.

"Saint, no. Relic, oh yes, yes."

"It is very holy, then?"

"Very holy, and also very unholy."

"What does that mean?"

A shrug of the shoulders. Evidently too difficult to explain.

"But you will keep it safe, Lady? Not let the Saracens take it. Very, very dangerous. Never open the box. Not Saracens, not Christians, nobody. Very, very dangerous."

"Then why do you bring it to us? It will be a danger to us, surely?"

"No danger to you, Lady. Only, do not open the box. Nobody open the box. No danger if the box is not opened."

"All right. We'll get a carpenter to nail it up."

At this he became agitated, and rolled his white-rimmed eyes.

"No, no. Shut with lock and key. Here is the key, you keep it," and he put the key into her hand. "Only, not use the key. Let the box stay shut. You will take it, Lady?"

There seemed no good reason to refuse, as she explained to the Abbess Jovetta. So, on Jovetta's behalf, the Abbess Hodierna accepted the strange gift, and watched two of the black priests carry it down into the cement cellars. It was a damp, cold, unpleasant spot, the cellar. Perhaps that was why, as they turned away, leaving the box in a convenient dark corner, the Abbess Hodierna suddenly felt a cold shudder come over her. It must be the place. It was a gloomy old spot.

The Coptic priests were fed, and sped on their way with gifts and blessings. The nuns pressed them to stay the night, but the priests were in haste. "Get away quick!" they said. "Saracens coming. You get away too. Hide your treasures."

But they could not tell them when the danger was to be, so the nuns blessed them, and saw them go off, silent, with bowed heads, into the night.

The Abbess of Shaston could not get that box out of her mind. After Compline, when all had retired to their cells, she lay wakeful, thinking about it. Pandora's Box? Oh, surely not that. That old story was long ago and far away. But wasn't she curious, just like Pandora? The priests had told her, so many times since she was a little girl, that curiosity was a sin, but she did not believe that. Curiosity — wanting to know, wanting to find out — how else could one learn? She had always given free rein to her curiosity, with the result that she knew a great many things, and was not afraid of knowing more.

So presently, finding the lure of a puzzle irresistible, the Abbess rose from her bed, dressed, took a taper, and passed through the dark floors of the convent, to the cellar. It was a night of bright moonlight — shafts of white brilliance cut through the arches of the cloisters, glinting like raindrops on the dry, polished surfaces of the palm leaves in the quadrangle gardens in the centre of each cloister. Not a leaf stirred there. Quietly though she walked, her footsteps woke the echoes. Those echoes woke to the slightest footfall, to a sigh, to a breath. But only her footsteps woke them now.

There were two floors of cloisters above the cellars, where the moonlight did not penetrate. The only light was thrown by the Abbess's little taper. Down the steps, and yes, here it was, the box of mystery. In the dim light of the taper she tried to make out the images that covered it: men, naked, with faces she did not like, and strange beasts. One figure took up most of the space on the lid. But it had been partially defaced — scratched, hacked and hammered. It was a tall, thin man, with a close hood round his face and a cloak hiding his shoulders and arms; the rest of his body seemed to be obliterated. Beneath where his feet should be, a rope, or a tail, seemed to be coiled, but the end of the rope too was obliterated.

She crouched down, fascinated. Then she took from the pocket of her robe the key which the priests had given her, and which she had not handed over to Jovetta. The key! With a feeling of tremulous excitement, she fitted the key into the lock and opened the box.

Something went past her, as if she had stumbled upon a nest of those foul flies that feed on unburied corpses. She put up her hands to ward it off. But she saw nothing, nor felt any insects, only a rushing, buzzing gust of air, and a loathsome smell. She had expected the mouldering smell of decay and neglect, but nothing like this. She recoiled, but it seemed to rush past her and was gone. Not yet daunted, she lifted her taper and peered into the box. Only an unidentifiable huddle of bones and rags, mostly fallen into dust. Not for anything would she have plunged her fingers into that dust to seek if there was anything beneath.

With a shudder, she closed the box, making sure the lid was fitted firmly down, and locked it with the key, which she slipped into her pocket. She made the sign of the cross over the box, traced a pentagram, and said a prayer for whatever soul had once inhabited those bones. Well, she reflected, whatever Presence had been in the box, it was gone now.

She went up the cellar steps, round three sides of a square in the lower cloister, and began to wonder whether she could have left something behind her — whether, in fact, she heard something. She would not permit herself to react — yet. Of course there was nothing following her. She was just a little shaken by that box, those bones. Very deliberately she ascended the stair to the upper cloisters. Two sides of a square to go round to her own apartments.

Yes, there was a sound behind her. Echoes of her own footsteps, of course. Like plodding, padding footsteps, stopping when she stopped. Echoes, of course. Yet not quite her pace. She looked back. Nothing, of course. She made a cross and a pentagram, and went on. She hastened her steps to see if the echoes would hasten too. They did not. They came on at the same slow pace. She found herself very unwilling to slacken her speed. Rather she hastened a little, a very little. Oh, she knew she must not start to run, or she would break into a panic. No, keep on, keep on, muttering those prayers that she could remember. It was with great relief that she reached her own door, stepped inside quickly, shut and bolted it, and dropped her hand into the holy water stoup by the doorpost. With the holy water she made seven crosses and five pentagrams, and did the same to every window, pipe, and vent-hole in her quarters. Only then did she feel safe enough to go to bed.

Another woman might have found comfort by telling herself that it was all a product of her imagination. But not the Abbess Hodierna. She knew too much, and what she knew was not comforting. The words of the Office of Compline kept recurring to her: "Because your adversary the Devil, as a roaring lion, goeth about, seeking whom he may devour . . ."

After a restless night she got up, unlatched her door, and looked out into the cloister. She repressed a cry. All along the cloister passageway was a track of footprints, in what seemed to be grey dust, as though a cat had trod in a flour-bin. Catlike. Yes, that was it, those catlike steps, but heavier, behind her last night. But these were huge — one, two, three, four toes, and the great pad in the centre. What kind of cat? "Like a lion, seeking whom he may devour." And the footprints stopped at her door.

With a shudder, she took a broom, and having first heavily sprinkled the dust with holy water and made the sign of the cross, hastily swept those footprints away.

She went to confession that morning, as indeed she was bound to do. She had a spiritual director, a nominal one, back in England, though in fact she obeyed no man's spiritual direction but the Pope's — if his. When abroad she chose a simple-minded parish priest, attached to the soldiers. She had no intention of asking his spiritual guidance, still less of telling him the secrets of her life. She required formal absolution, and she made a formal confession.

She told the priest that she had yielded to the sin of curiosity, and handled something that did not belong to her. She had opened a forbidden box.

"And what was in the box?"

"Rags and bones and dust, nothing more."

"And did anything come out of the box?"

"Only a swarm of flies."

"Well, well . . . ." He considered. "Was it the relic of a saint, do you think?"

"No, the Coptic priests said it was not a saint."

"And did you take anything away?"

"No, nothing. I closed the box and locked it. I kept only the key, and that I gave back to the Abbess

Jovetta." (So she had done, but without mentioning that she had used it.)

"Well, well. I do not think there was any very great sin there, save that of curiosity." And he gave her a light penance, and a formal absolution.

Later in the afternoon, she was approached by three of the "pupillae." These, "little dolls," or "babies," were girls of good family, who boarded in the convent, and learnt good manners along with religion, sewing, embroidery, singing, and the rudiments of Latin, and not much else. They were all charming children, but three — Alys, Eleanor, and Jeanne — were particularly delightful. They were about eleven years old, and being prepared for their First Communion in a few weeks. Now, looking serious and worried, they approached the Abbess.

"Reverend Mother, oh, Reverend Mother," said Alys, who had been pushed forward by the others, "can we speak to you? We're — we're worried."

"Certainly, little one. But why don't you go to your own Abbess? I'm only a visitor here, you know."

"Yes, we know, but . . . it's not easy to talk to her." (The Abbess Hodierna smiled to herself.) "We don't think she'd listen to us. It's — we're frightened."

The Abbess drew in her breath sharply.

"Well, tell me, little ones. What frightened you?"

"We think — we think we saw a man from our window last night."

"Of course we know," Eleanor hastily put in, "we ought not to have been looking out of the window.

I *know* we ought to have been in bed. But it was a lovely night, and we got out of bed and went to the big window at the end of the corridor."

"That's why we don't want to tell Mother Abbess," put in Jeanne.

"Yes, I see. Well, go on. What did you see?"

"It looks into the big vegetable garden. Well, as we were looking out, a man came along the path. We don't know how he got in — and — and — he wasn't like a proper man at all. He wore a hood and cloak, down the length of his arms. But below that, his legs were like lions' legs, and he'd a tail — a long tail that trailed on the ground."

"With a great tuft at the end of it," Jeanne said.

"He walked right round the garden," Alys went on. "We all saw him, though we couldn't see his face. And then he went . . ."

"Which way did he go?" the Abbess asked.

"Oh, we *think* he went round the side of the house. We couldn't see him after that. Reverend Mother, we didn't like the look of him at all."

"No wonder you didn't," said the Abbess. "Well, my dears, I'll bless you as strongly as ever I can. Say your prayers very diligently. There's nothing much else I can advise you to do. No, I'm afraid your own Reverend Mother must be told, but I'll tell her, and I'll see that she doesn't blame you. After all, if no one had been looking out of the window, this man, or whatever it is, wouldn't have been seen by anyone."

She blessed them, and invoked many protections on them that were not in the Mass-book, and then sent them on their way. They were so fresh and innocent, she reflected — oh, certainly not angels, and when they were not on their best behaviour, just as much little devils of mischief as the next child, and just as vexatious to their poor Sister-Tutor. But for all that, their young faces made her heart turn over. She was the Notorious Abbess, always challenging danger and getting away with it, but they — God forbid that the thing in the garden should lay its fingers on them.

"No, of course I'll not punish them," the Abbess Jovetta said. "But they must be guarded. A senior Sister by the dormitory window, and another in the cloister. No more peering out of the windows by night. And we'll get the gardeners and the huntsman to patrol the grounds. I can quite believe there's been a man skulking about, but all that about lion's feet and a tail — well, Hodierna, surely you know what to make of that. Childish imagination, nothing more."

It would be no use, the Abbess Hodierna reflected, to tell her about the footprints, or about what came out of the box.

"But just in case there *is* something infernal," the Abbess Jovetta went on, "I'll send for Father Joseph from the Benedictines tomorrow and ask him to do an exorcism."

"Why not tonight?"

"Oh, heavens, it's nearly Vespers already, and this is no time to be fetching a man out. Besides, there's no one handy to send. Tomorrow will have to do."

"Fair enough. But I hope tomorrow won't be too late."

So how to keep watch? There were so many ways by which the lion-footed thing could come. The Abbess thought of trying to see all the corners of the convent simultaneously, by using her crying mirror; but she felt that that might be opening the door too widely to unknown influences. Things — Powers — had been known to get in through magic mirrors.

So, horribly against her will, she chose the place which the thing would be the most likely to regard as home — that cellar. With holy water and a crucifix, and wrapped in a dark thick cloak against the chills of the night and the dampness of the place, she sat herself down that night on a low stool in the cellar, close to that sinister box, and waited. It was now after Compline. "Brethren, be sober, be vigilant, because your adversary, the Devil. . . ."

Rigid and upright, like a black statue covered with her black mantle, she sat, her hands crossed on her breast, one hand clutching the crucifix with its attached rosary entwined round her wrist so she could not lose it; the other hand holding the flask of holy water; like Osiris whose crossed arms hold the crook and flail. As she sat, she heard a sound, a sound as of something coming toward her — padding, feline footsteps and the sound of something dragging. It came through the door, and instantly she was on the alert. Then she saw them. First the man in the hood, his hands doubled under his cloak as though with the effort of dragging something behind him, his head down. She could see neither his face nor his hands. But his legs below the cloak — yes, they were lion's legs, huge and out of proportion to his thin shoulders and small head. The head was no broader than one of the thick haunches, and the great spreading paws, with the talons, seemed to be larger than the rest of the creature's whole body. Obscenely placed over the loins was what seemed like another face; and the creature's long tail, like a rope, stretched out behind it, prehensile. The victim it was dragging was poor little Alys. Her hands, clasped in front of her, were encircled by a double coil of that pale, hairless tail, from the tassel of which yet another face peered up. She shuffled along, in her white shift, like a captive of war, not resisting, at least not physically. She seemed to be unconscious. In the dim light of the Abbess's one candle they passed by her, neither the victim nor the tormentor seeming to see her. They appeared to be going deeper into the dark recess at the back of the cellar. There was another passage there, leading nobody knew whither.

For a moment the Abbess was too horrified to move, and in that moment they had passed her. But she sprang to her feet, with the rosary hanging from her right wrist and the holy water bottle clutched in her right hand. With her left she caught up the candle, and followed them. They were moving faster than she thought. She had to run to keep up with them. At last, getting within reach, she dashed the holy water over the creature, uttering the strongest imprecation of power that she knew.

The creature turned its head, looked at her, snarled and spat, and went on. Alys, stumbling forward, emitted a moan. They went on. They were in another room now, the oldest chamber of the cellars, vaulted like the crypt of a church, dead dark save for the Abbess's quivering candle. It cast the shadow of Alys on the stone-flagged floor, but the creature cast no shadow at all. The Abbess prayed, formed the sign of the cross, but all to no avail. Then desperate and forgetting all else, she rushed forward, threw her arm, with the rosary and the crucifix, round Alys, and with her left hand thrust the candle into the monstrous little face on the creature's tail. It shrieked in a high shrill voice, and loosened its hold. The Abbess gathered up Alys, throwing off the slackened coils of the tail. The crucifix was now between Alys and the Creature. The candle had spun out of the Abbess's hand, but had not gone out. She commended herself and the child to God and the

Holy Angels, and waited, hearing the beast hissing and panting in the dark, within an arm's length.

Then a voice spoke, heavy, dark, leaden.

"Give me that child. Asmodeus, you have done your work. You may go. You, woman, give me that child."

From a mouth dry with panic, the Abbess said into the darkness: "No."

The darkness thinned a little, and she saw a great and terrible Presence. It sat on a high throne, and was gigantic in size — far, far larger than the stone chamber — filling the sky and all the conscious world. In shape it was like a great goat, but with a man's head, arms, and body. The face was as of one old, withered, drawn — a long nose, a long chin, pouched eyes, drooping wrinkles, straggling beard — a face of old iniquity, joyless and pitiless. Great goat-horns spiralled up from the brows, above the ears of a goat, and between the horns, a thick black candle stood burning. Strong cruel hands grasped the hand-rests of the great throne, and the feet, cloven-shaped, were firmly planted on the steps below, and seemed to be trampling—what? Whatever it was, it bled.

"Give me that child," the Presence said again.

"No."

"I tell you, it will be the worse for you. You weak thing, do you think you can defy me? Just because you have met one of my emissaries and got off safely from the encounter, do you think you have over-come — Me? You do not know what I am. Your painted devils in psalters, your hell-mouths in coloured glass, what are they but my small servants, like that Asmodeus who brought you here. For I am the Great Darkness, older and greater than Light. I am Chaos and Not-Being, the Everlasting No. Puny little sorceress, dabbling in spells, do you see what you have challenged?"

In an extremity of terror, she said, in a small trembling voice, "Yet you cannot take this child unless I give her up. The crucifix defeats you." She held the crucifix as firmly as she could against the child's body, between her and the Dark Power.

He gave a scornful laugh. "It pleases you to think so. But I have powers I could put forth against *you*. First your body. I can send you back to your life, smitten with loathsome diseases, painful. You would live for years, and every minute would be a different agony, a new one beginning as soon as custom had hardened you to the old. You would become foul, so that those who had to tend you could not bear to come nigh you. Years and long years, and still not able to die. Is it enough? Then give me the child."

"What," she said, looking him in his terrible yellow goat-eyes, "will you do with her?"

"Oh, not much harm. I would only change her a little. Send her back to her friends — oh, with her body quite unharmed, but her mind changed, ever such a little. There she would remain with them, like a seed of my planting, to increase and bear fruit for me."

"You accursed demon of the pit!" She began to find her voice again through sheer anger. "Not if you tortured every fibre of this poor body. Not even then will I give her up. Do your worst!"

"Indeed?" A kind of grim amusement without geniality came into his voice. "My worst! I think you have no idea how bad that can be. Not only your body — your mind. Perhaps you would prefer to become a mindless thing, not speaking or thinking or moving, just witnessing your own helplessness? Or would you prefer to be visited with terrors and madness, shrieking horrors driving you from nightmare to nightmare, but unable either to awake or to sleep?"

"Not even for that. Oh God, all things are in Thy hand. Let me endure what I must. Fiend, I still defy you."

The dark figure made no reply.

The Abbess cried aloud, "Guardian Angel, come to me now." But nothing stirred in reply.

"He will not come," said the fiend. "You have tempted him once too often." And the gleaming yellow eyes held hers, and grew larger and larger. Then Alys stirred in her arms and gave a little plaintive sound. It drew her eyes away from the Fiend's, and she looked at the crucifix in her hand, held fast against the child's side. Suddenly a great sob burst from her.

"Oh, my God, forgive my pride, and accept my humiliation." She bowed herself close above the crucifix. "In my pride I have sought to wield power in my own strength. It was pride, and now I am humbled. Lord my God, I deserve no mercy. Cast me off, condemn me, grind me into the uttermost pit of damnation, but save the child!"

"Who are you praying to?" said the Fiend. "To your God? But your God is dead. Your God will not save you. He cannot. Your soul is already mine. Look at me —" and once again he drew her eyes to his, and the dark slit pupils expanded, expanded. "Your God is dead. Give me the child!"

She drew her eyes away.

"No," she exclaimed. "Every word you say is a lie. You are the Father of Lies, and I do not believe you. Even if my God were dead, He would rise again. You have no power over me, nor over this child here. You know, for you also believe and tremble."

Far behind her she heard a bell, and a far-off sound of singing. A light over her shoulder lit upon the Great Devil on his great throne and changed all the colours of the apparition. For a moment he stood there, without his throne, a grey horned figure, larger than human, with battle wings outspread — the wall behind him was transparent, with the hills and the sky visible beyond. Then the horned man shrank in size, paled in colour, flung out his hands in